KU-311-298

CAVAN COUNTY LIBRARY
ACC No
CLASS No
INVOICE NO
PRICE

THE EMERALD LIE

A JACK TAYLOR NOVEL

KEN BRUEN

LARGE PRINT

First published in the United States of America

CAVAN COUNTY LIBRARY
ACC No. S/3187
CLASS NO F Large Print
INVOICE NO 10536 Wuers
PRICE £27.95

First Isis Edition
published 2017
by arrangement with
Abner Stein

The moral right of the author has been asserted

Copyright © 2016 by Ken Bruen
All rights reserved

A catalogue record for this book is available
from the British Library.

ISBN 978–1–78541–427–5 (hb)
ISBN 978–1–78541–433–6 (pb)

Published by
F. A. Thorpe (Publishing)
Anstey, Leicestershire

Set by Words & Graphics Ltd.
Anstey, Leicestershire
Printed and bound in Great Britain by
T. J. International Ltd., Padstow, Cornwall

This book is printed on acid-free paper

For
Aine and David O Connor
Heroic in a gentle way
and
Marvin Minkler
A true star

Lance Armstrong: "Everybody wants to know what I'm on. What am I on? I'm on my bike, busting my balls six hours a day. What are you on?"
"Grammar!"

Tom Darcy was giving it large about van Graal, the new manager of Man United. He wasn't shouting.

Yet.

But he was very loud and verging on aggressive. Like this:

"You have to remember Ferguson wasn't successful when he started."

His companion, a small man with a small tone, nodded, staring into his pint, hoping it might help.

It didn't.

Darcy finished his third Jameson, belched, said,

"See, managers *do be* playing the long game."

A man farther along the bar, dressed in a black denim shirt, black jeans, visibly blanched. He had a long slender face with a slight scar above the right eye and it seemed to twitch now in annoyance. He lifted his tonic water, took a bitter sip. He wanted a double gin but it could wait. Duty must. Darcy said, more roared,

"Gotta point Percy at the porcelain."

The man didn't look but he was fairly sure that Darcy winked. He took a deep breath then followed Darcy. Darcy was zipping up then moved to wash his

3

large hands. He clocked the man enter but he knew not to make eye contact in a men's lavatory.

Thought,

"WTF?"

As the man stood right by the basin, he snapped,

"Help yah?"

(Not full on but enough to let menace spill over the tone.)

The man seemed to focus, as if collating thoughts, then,

"The Yahoos that make up this city, they can tell you the offside rule but as to what a split infinitive is? Forget it. Now when you were rather haranguing your comrade at the bar, you said . . ."

He paused, as if ensuring he got it correct, then,

"*Do be!*"

Darcy laughed, a mix of relief and disbelief, this punter was simply another nutter in a city chockablock with madness. He leaned back, mocked,

"Dooby do bee do."

The man lashed out with his right hand, throwing Darcy back against the wall, intoned,

"You cretin, you mock? Grammar is with us from the fifth century BC, from India. You probably think the great subcontinent gave us bus conductors and curry. When language is corrupted, it is but a small step to chaos. Look at

X Factor

Fifty Shades of Grey

chick lit

and . . ."

4

He had to catch a breath, such was his indignation, then,

"Texting."

He grabbed Darcy by his hair and began to systematically smash his face against the porcelain bowl, and in an almost singsong voice, said,

"*I* before *e* but not after . . ."

He was still reeling off the rules as his hand released the limp body, which slid to the floor. He looked down at it, as if surprised to see it, then, sighing, pulled himself together, said,

"The center cannot hold."

He took a single white card from his jacket, laid it almost reverently atop the destroyed face. It had one letter, in bold black:

A

Extra adverbs, used for emphasis, are called intensifiers.

E.g . . . he was very dead.

Superintendent Clancy was as close to apoplexy as it is possible to get short of a brain hemorrhage. Lined before him was the Murder Unit. Among them was the newly promoted Sergeant Ni Iomaire, Ridge. A former ally of Jack Taylor, a rarity in the Guards, openly gay and feisty. Her friendship/alliance with Jack had cost her dear in the past but two years of no contact had fast-tracked her career. Behind her back, she was called, to rhyme with *Inspector Gadget*,

Inspector Faggot.

Clancy too had once been a close friend of Jack's but was now his archenemy. He roared at the collected detectives,

"A second murder, the week before the Galway Races?"

The Races mattered; the killings, not so much. He said,

"And the only lead is the cards he leaves on the bodies?"

He had to check his notes, read,

"An *a* and an *e*? The sweet Jesus is that about?"

Ridge said,

"Vowels, sir."

He gave her the Look. He'd picked it up from watching *The Armstrong Lie*. He said in an icy low tone,

"Don't fucking tell me he's working through the vowels?"

Pause.

"Is he going to start on the frigging consonants next?"

The second murder had happened on the promenade in Salthill. In full view of crowds. Many ... many witnesses described the killer as

White

Tall

Short

Muslim

A woman

A gang!

Had a small scar under his eye.

A man had been standing right on the edge of the footpath, arguing with somebody, and when the other person left, he'd been approached by a figure who said some words to him, then literally

... *threw him under the bus.*

One witness said,

"It was as if he was waiting for the No. 24 from Eyre Square, then pushed hard and the victim went under the wheels. The pusher had stopped for a moment, then casually walked over and dropped a white card on the mangled remains, turned, and sauntered away."

Clancy said,

"Whatever else, he's a brazen bollix."
Now the super glared at his troops, asked,
"So, thoughts?"
A thick former hurler from Thurles tried,
"He knows his bus times."
And another wag threw in,
"Least we know the buses are running on time."
Not smart.
Clancy had left his sense of humor in 1988. He snapped at the wag,
"Take your smart mouth and canvass all the houses along the prom, and I mean all of them."
A groan.
This was usually a tedious task for a uniform. Now Clancy asked,
"Any more bright sparks?"
Ridge ventured,
"Do the cards tell us anything? Prints, where they were bought?"
A nod from Clancy, then,
"Get on it."

I had been given a Labrador pup after my last case. I'd given him a red-and-white bandanna for the Galway team and for Willie Nelson. He whimpered if I didn't wrap it around him at night. I was going to name him Boru for a departed friend and so he might choose his battles carefully but then, like my life, went with

"Storm."

Not so much in a teacup as in situ.

In truth I had determined to stay detached from him, not to spare the love but to keep at a distance, like modern parenting. Not that I was necessarily a cold cunt but to protect myself. There was a previous dog whose horrendous death I had to keep at a remove even today. I was still raw from the discovery in my home of his torn remains.

But dogs . . .

Go figure

Have other plans.

Slowly Storm had melted away my resolve. Most evenings we went to feed the swans and round off that walk by sitting on the rocks and staring at the Atlantic Ocean. The whole of Galway Bay before us, I'd take out my flask of Jameson, have a few considered nips, and I'd be able to let my breath out. Storm slowly chewed his rationed treats. Finally I'd light my one and only daily cigarette, stare at the horizon, and yearn.

For what?

Fuck knows?

Storm would place one paw on my knee. Such tiny gestures signifying, if not hope, then a slanted comfort. Ease from left field as it were. To my back were the remnants of Seapoint. Once a vast ballroom, it was the center of all the social outlet in the city, home to the show bands. A whole generation had grown up with them, my generation, dying slowly and forever.

The Royal

The Capital

Dixies

And even the wonderfully non-PC

The Indians.

Man, I loved those days.

A singer from Belfast then, no Van but David McWilliams, had a fine tune,

"The Days of Pearly Spencer."

Summed it all up.

Then.

That the PC brigade were still pursuing the Indians to change their name was a measure of just how much we had lost our sense of fun over the years.

An elderly Bohermore woman summed it up:

"You're afraid to open your mouth these days."

As Israel and Hamas continued to add to a daily number of deaths and no sign of peace, yet another airline went down, Putin continued to wreak havoc in the Ukraine, Bill Clinton was yet again accused of affairs, the country tried to delight in five Garth Brooks concerts. But one asshole councillor in Dublin managed to derail them, depriving the people of the only hope of a bit of fun they'd had in years. Not to mention the loss of fifty million to the country in revenue.

Enda Kenny, our leader, was the most despised man in the nation. He smirked daily over water charges, Garth Brooks, and just about any issue that was of note to his population.

Our former tone of humor was now replaced by an all-prevalent fear as medical cards were canceled, bankers walked free after hugely expensive trials, but one woman stood tall. An ordinary housewife, she had been systemically abused as a child and for fifteen years sought redress. Even after the supreme court turned her down, she persisted with frail strength all the way to the European Court of Justice.

And won.

A small brave lady.

The government set up *a committee* to gauge whether she merited an apology.

A collective,

. . . *for fucksake*

From everybody: well, everybody of basic human decency.

Just before the Galway Races kicked off, I got a call from the arts editor of the *Galway Advertiser*, Kernan Andrews, asking me to do an interview. Kernan was one of the good guys. He was doing a series, "Faces of Galway."

I figured I was under the subheading:

"Battered Faces of Galway."

What the hell, I'd get to sit down with Kernan, sink a few, shoot the shit. We arranged to meet in Garavan's. Grab the snug there and have if not privacy at least a certain amount of atmosphere. I recently had a new neighbor, an ex-army guy and — whisper it — *British army*.

Why you would retire to a Republican stronghold was beyond me. But he kept a low profile and his accent under wraps. We had shared a dram or two and he seemed to like Storm real well and when I had to get out alone, he would always be delighted to mind the pup. His name was

Charles Stokes.

He was usually addressed as Doc.

A good, no-frills UK name.

He'd done a stint in Northern Ireland and knew I had, let's say, dealings over the border, but we had reached our own separate peace and, whatever flags we flew under, we had an appreciation of fine malt and Jameson. I brought the pup over to him early on the Friday morning, said,

"Believe it or not, I'm being interviewed."

He was tall with a shock of steel to white hair, riveting stare with nigh on nonbreak hold. He adopted a very dry droll sense of humor. Said,

"Not helping with enquiries, one hopes."

I handed over the pup's dinner bowl and his cherished bandanna, said,

"Nope, an actual bona fide gig."

He rubbed the dog, said,

"Talk as if you believed it."

"Always end the name of your child with a vowel so that when you yell the name will carry." (Bill Cosby)

As I said, Kernan is one of the good guys. Looks like a roadie for a heavy metal band and beneath a mellow, affable facade beats a mind as smart as a whip. We met in Freeneys, a slice of old Galway, unchanged and in the window they sell fishing tackle. I'd managed to procure for him a signed Barcelona shirt with the 2010 team names. Cost me . . . oh, some serious weight. In truth, I'd traded my 1963 All Ireland Galway Football shirt for it.

Phew-oh.

Loved that shirt, was even signed. Kernan greeted me warmly.

"So glad you agreed to do this, Jack."

He was dressed as always as if en route to the ever-running Dylan tour. I'd worn my all-weather Garda coat, item 1834, that the Department of Justice even now wrote demanding back. I said,

"Buddy, hear my answers and then see how glad you are."

He smiled. My acid tongue was part of the reason he liked me. The bar guy, Willy, knew us and asked,

"What will it be, lads?"

Sparkling water for Kernan and Jameson back for me. The gig lasted two hours and I haven't said so much since Charles Haughey was shunted from office.

I list some of the more pertinent questions.

K: "So, Jack, any heroes?"

J: ". . . Once, in my naive days, I thought a lot of Lance Armstrong."

"You're kidding."

"Sure, it wasn't so much I knew a lot about cycling but I did, in an old Galway way, admire endurance."

Kernan let that slide, tried,

"How would you like to be remembered?"

"As a fine hurler."

Kernan . . . sigh.

The interview had some key questions.

"What are you reading now?"

"Cycle of Lies, Juliet Macur, and Wheelmen, the definitive accounts of the whole doping mess."

Kernan had opted to create an interview that balanced the solemn with the fun, as in,

"Where do you get your . . . um . . . distinctive wardrobe?"

"The charity shops."

Then,

"Have you still got passions?"

"Sure, books, my dog, and a new fascination with the Tour de France."

"What is your most prized possession?"

"My father's hurley, hewn from the original ash."

"Do you still play?"

"Only in the alleyways and back streets and not a referee in sight."

"Where do you stand on the Church?"

I laughed.

"More like the Church tries to stand on me. I see them as the ecclesiastical wing of Enron."

I pronounced the last word wrong to draw out the sense of nonsense.

"Is there a significant other in your life?"

Here he paused, gave a small smile, warned,

"And I don't mean your dog."

"The person I am in most contact with is the Inland Revenue bollocks."

"Will you ever leave Galway?"

I went with the half-formed truth.

"In Corsica, there is a lovely town, Bastia, and I have made inroads there with a man named Sabatini to buy a small villa."

Kernan was skeptical, rightly so in light of my history.

I had left Ireland as often as the government did a decent thing. He asked,

"They serve Jameson there?"

I let that slide.

Then the semi-frivolous

"What are you reading, Jack?"

"Jason Starr, Gerard Brennan, Hilary Davidson, Eoin Colfer."

"And music?"

"Johnny Duhan and Marc Roberts."

"TV?"

"Lot of documentaries."
Enron
The Armstrong Lie
Paul Kimmage, *Rough Rider*
Meet the Mormons
Conspiracy
And of course, *Spiral, Luck, Orange Is the New Black, The Killing* (Season 4), and revisited some movies:
Killing Them Softly
The Insider
I then tore the arse out of the government over medical cards, water charges, and all the other despicable acts they laid on us daily. We finished up after that and, of course, a day later I would think of many witty wise remarks I could, should have said but, like the Church, it was all smoke. As Kernan prepared to leave, he stopped, asked,

"Whatever happened to that girl, Emily, you were hanging with for a bit?"

Indeed.

Green hell.

Phew-oh.

Where to begin?

Times are, a person comes into your life and maybe enriches it, or adds to it, then there are those who simply disrupt your balance. The third kind blitzkrieg into your existence and shatter every possible level of your being.

Such was Emerald/Emily, and many other aliases in between. Half girl, most ways lethal woman. A

20

homicidal, compassionate, funny, mad bitch of a dervish who truly defies easy categorization. Think Becky Sharp, crossed with Scarlett O'Hara, sprinkled with Larsson's Lisbeth Salander, and topped off with Carol O'Connell's Mallory.

Even thus, I sell her short.

Not one day did she appear in the same guise, never mind the same personality. She told me she laid out identities on her bed in the morning like clothes and slipped into whatever character was waiting. Be it

Helpful

Murderous

Hilarious

Maddening

Aggressive

And true, she got me out of all kinds of deep shite and as she did so, dropped me into chasms of utter dismay. My pup Storm was a gift from her. She may or may not have killed her father and a psycho who had torn my previous dog to bits.

I felt for her:

Love

Hatred

Affection

Consternation

Admiration

And she preyed on my mind like mild paranoia. Then she simply upped and disappeared, leaving an e-mail address

. . . greenhell@gmail.com

During the time she'd been in my life, she crossed paths with my ex-friend and ally Garda Ridge. Newly promoted to sergeant. They had gone to it like soured sisters, and on points I'd have to concede that Emily won. Ridge only referred to her as

. . . *psycho bitch*.

Like that.

Not a whole lot of love riffing. Emily's father, a nasty piece of shit, had been a major player in academic circles and was suspected of multiple assaults, perhaps even murder of young students. He was found with a nail in his head. For a time I was lead suspect and Emily provided a highly dubious but unbreakable alibi. Further not endearing her to Sergeant Ridge.

I strongly suspected that one dark day Emily would be back on the scene. Something about the Galway air had lodged in her bones and she sure did love to mind-fuck the city. Too, her alcoholic mother still lived on the outskirts of town, not that Emily actually gave a sweet fuck about her but she did like the family home. Had said,

"I'd like to inherit the family residence."

Surprised, I'd replied,

"Didn't really figure sentiment in your agenda."

She gave that laugh that no matter how infuriating she was, you couldn't help but warm to her. She had looked me right in the eye and said,

"I want to see it burn."

While I was in mid-interview, the Grammarian was adding the letter *i* to his murderous list. This time, he offed a teenager at the Galway docks. A cruise ship had tried to dock but the port couldn't handle the size and the two hundred or so shop-anxious passengers who might have been ferried to the shore to satisfy their retail mania had to simmer on deck as the rain came lashing down and this cost the city a small fortune in lost sales. The Dublin council would come in for another whipping but this was par for its muddled course. An asshole running the council refused to budge on the Garth Brooks concerts, stonewalling the five concerts due to give the country a badly needed uplift.

There was even a personal plea by Garth, who begged the Taoiseach, saying,

"I will crawl on my hands and knees if that is what it takes but let the people have a party."

Enda Kenny, as was now his wont, showed total scorn for the population and rebuffed the offer in just about as rude a fashion as he could muster.

And . . . with that knowing smirk he usually reserved for when he was threatening us with the water charges. It would cost the nation nigh on fifty-six million in lost revenue, not to mention the goodwill of close to a million voters.

The teenager mentioned above had pushed an elderly man, sneering,

"Outta my way, yah old fuck."

The Grammarian had moved right in and shot the idiot in the back of the head. And strolled away. He was dressed in a blue overall and carrying a clipboard. The ultimate disguise.

Superintendent Clancy had gone ballistic.

"In front of a cruise ship of Yanks?"

. . . as if that were the real crime.

Ridge was given a whole new arsehole after he had reamed her and told her to catch this perp or go back to uniform.

The Galway Races came and I backed a horse named Road to Riches who won at six to one, giving my account in Bank of Ireland some credibility. I meanwhile continued to walk the dog and had taken a new and odd route to reading. I was letting each book lead to another direction. For example, the Lance Armstrong book led me to *Double Down*, a fascinating account of the 2012 U.S. election. Which brought me to Joe McGinniss's book on Sarah Palin, which led me to *Freakonomics*, and thus back to Nick Kent with his superb book on music, *Apathy for the Devil*.

I don't quite know what this speaks to regarding my state of mind save to suggest I was befuddled but highly engaged.

And then I collapsed. Right on Shop Street. The frigging shame. One minute I was considering having a pint in Garavan's then next I am on my back, staring at the gray sky, wondering,

"How the fuck did that happen?"

Result, I spent three days in hospital. My only visitor was my next-door neighbor. The Guards had come round and told him my arse was stretched. He brought grapes, if not of wrath, at least of thoughtfulness. And

Essential.

"A bottle of Seven-Up."

24

Yeah, right.

It was in that bottle but was 58 proof. He said,

"A pick-me-up."

And he was taking the dog for walks and feeding the mite. Said,

"He's pining for you."

I smiled, said,

"He'd be the first."

He gave a rueful nod, then,

"Sure that's not so."

I managed to sit up despite the line of tubes and shite they had trailing out of me, said,

"Not self-pity, it's just that every close friend I had got burned."

He laughed.

"Sounds like you're warning me off."

"Fuck no, you mind my dog, you are gold, my man."

True that.

I had a serious fright on my second day in hospital, the doctors saying they had to do some tests. You hear that, don't make plans. Did I worry?

Did I fuck.

I had two crushed fingers, fucked hearing, a limp, and damn nigh every addiction guaranteed to shorten your days. So, no, optimistic I wasn't. Would I go the Walter White route and undergo heavy treatment?

Nope.

I hadn't the balls but I did bargain.

You grow up Catholic, you still think you have options. I said to God,

"Give me a reprieve and I'll . . ."

. . . What?

"Go to confession."

Phew-oh.

Nearly enough to wish for a bad result.

I got the good news.

Clear.

Not that I didn't get the full-on lecture: change habits; eat vegan; no booze, cigs, or indeed anything worth breathing for. Winding up, the doctor said,

"You should be dead, the way you have treated your system. You are one lucky man."

I smiled, said,

"Oh, yeah, lucky, that's me."

They used to say that any day you can wake up and eat a boiled egg you are ahead of the game. I hate fucking eggs. On my way back from the hospital, I stopped at the cathedral, looked in vain for a list of confession times. In my youth, Saturday night, the whole town lined up for the ordeal of weekly confession. Everyone tried to avoid Father Healy. He was one biblical bastard and you never got out without the very wrath of God in your ears. And he was loud. You'd hear, as some poor bollix withered in his box,

"You beat your wife, you neglected your children, you disgrace the very faith you profess."

Then there was Father Neill, a soft touch. He let you off with a quiet penance of six Hail Marys. You could see the lines outside his box, no one at Healy's. I was staring at a confessional when a priest approached. In his late fifties, he looked cowed. Most did nowadays.

The lynch mob wasn't exactly at the gate but hovering. He asked,

"May I be of some service?"

This new gentle diplomacy was hard to stomach. When you'd grown up with Gestapo-like fucks ruling the parish, it was difficult to turn on sixpence. I said,

"Don't they post times of confession anymore?"

He gave a sad smile, said,

"It's called the sacrament of reconciliation now."

I shook my head, asked,

"And does it, you know, reconcile?"

He nearly smiled but bit down on it, put out his hand, said,

"I'm Father Thomas."

"Jack, Jack Taylor."

A light in his eyes, then,

"Weren't you recently in the paper?"

Fame.

Or if a priest recognizes you, perhaps infamy. I nodded, and he indicated I could sit . . . or maybe kneel because those days were long over. He said,

"Perhaps I could help you?"

I was already planning how to get the fuck out of there without fuss, said,

"Thank you for your time . . ." (I just couldn't use *Father*) "Tom."

"Thomas."

I nearly laughed, snapped,

"Still with the corrections I see."

He caught himself, tried,

"I didn't mean . . . what I wanted to offer was if you wished me to hear your . . ."

Now he didn't know what to call it. I let him off, said,

"Naw, I figure I'll live with the gig I'm playing."

I reached into my wallet, handed over a rash of notes. He made a feeble gesture of protest, said,

"There's no need, I haven't done anything."

I was at the door when I said,

"And right there is the reason you guys are hiding out."

I dipped my hand in the holy water font but it was empty. Seemed apt.

I'd barely got to Salmon Weir Bridge where all the fish had long since ceased jumping, poisoned like the country, when a homeless guy approached, with, I have to say, attitude, thinking,

"This shuck came out of the church, got to be good for piety."

Figured wrong.

He pushed,

"Gimme something for a meal."

"Why?"

Stymied him but he rallied.

"Because I'm suffering."

"Me, too," I said.

"This is the sort of English up with which I will not put." (Winston Churchill)

I was having a breakfast of sorts in the GBC. Still the only old-style restaurant in the city and with prices that were reasonable. The cook, Frank Casserly, came out to say hello and asked,

"Fry-up?"

Indeed.

This was

Two sausages

Two fried eggs

Two rashers

And thick-cut slices of bread.

No black pudding or beans.

My doctor would have had a coronary. Sometimes you just have to fuck with a diagnosis. My food arrived as a man approached my table. He asked,

"May I join you?"

Looked at my food, said,

"Not really."

He sat, said,

"I won't need long."

I had just started on the bacon when he slid a manila envelope across the table. I snapped,

"Hey, if I wanted company I'd have brought my dog."

He was in his late fifties, good suit, remnants of a tan, groomed silver hair, but an air of pain, as if he'd been recently bereaved. That look I know. I finished the food, began on the tea, than picked up the envelope, asked,

"Is this going to piss me off?"

An expression lit across his eyes, fleeting but I saw it, utter horror. He said,

"It's my daughter, Karen."

A beautiful girl in a graduation mortarboard and gown, had that classic Irish look, the dark eyes, dark hair, and bold expression. I said,

"She's a beauty; is she missing?"

I kept my tone neutral, as if it mattered not a jot.

He said,

"My name is Tom Shea, I run the accountant firm near the courthouse."

I knew them, players.

Then he reached into his jacket, produced a sheaf of photos, said,

"This is her . . ."

A beat.

"After."

I did not want to see. I knew it would be bad and I knew even more that I did not want any part of it. I had enough money not to have to worry for a time and I was so wrecked by the last years of

Utter devastation

That I had no energy for anything but walking the dog. He whispered,

"Please."

Fuck.

I took the photos and scanned them, my breakfast rebelled, tried to repeat, I said,

"Holy Jesus."

They were bad; no, awful in the biblical sense. I had seen mutilations, batterings, torture, but this was new.

New in its complete

Butchery

Savagery, black dark evil.

He nodded.

I had no words. What can you possibly say when you are faced with the very worst that humanity has served up? A long tense minute passed and I stood, said,

"I'm going to need a drink and to throw up, just not sure what the sequence is going to be." I paid, in a sort of numbed shell, left a decent tip for Frank and Cecily, and headed out into bright sunlight. It should have been dark, with all the theatrical attendants. He was right behind me. I stopped, asked,

"Have you got a cigarette?"

Ridiculous. He had all the look of a health guy, leastways before the photos. He shook his head so we crossed the road to Hollands. Mary, God bless her, was still working there. She beamed.

"Jack."

I muttered some lame hello, nearly asked for her mother but had heard somewhere that the poor woman had recently passed. I said,

"Pack of Major, love"

We went to Garavan's. I ordered a pint and chaser. Shea said he'd have a sparkling water, adding,

"I start to drink, I'm gone."

Looked pretty gone as it was. We didn't talk until I got on the heavy side of the drinks and finally let a breath out, said,

"Tell me."

He was staring at the bubbles in the water, watching them dance, then,

"She was final year in NUIG. Like a lot of girls, she worked at various jobs for pocket money. She was told about a company doing videos for companies, supposed to be some sort of inspirational shit, like training videos. And hey, maybe some TV work."

Sighed deeply, said,

"And everybody wants to be a star, right?"

He had to bite down, then,

"Real Time Inc., that's the name, cover for torture porn. East European crew, led by a smart-mouth Yank name of Fletcher."

I had to ask,

"The Guards?"

"Nothing they could do, no proof."

"Where is she now, Karen?"

"A coffin."

Fuck.

I had no idea what he wanted from me. He knew who did it. The Guards were useless. Not that I could tell him to move on or any other Oprah horseshit. As if reading my mind, he said,

34

"I checked you out. You haven't always worked within regulations."

Meaning, I went rogue, took justice to the alleys. I didn't have what it took to take the road again. He added,

"A few friends of mine are going to, um . . .

He searched for an efficient way of conveying *vigilantes*. I knew the signs. I'd been down this road in a very bloody fashion before. Vigilantes started out with maybe . . . maybe . . . a semblance of righteousness but always descended into mayhem. He continued,

"Find another solution."

"Why do you need me?"

"They are unfamiliar with the territory."

I knew he meant geographically and certainly not peacefully. Before I could answer, he added,

"I will of course be paying you handsomely for your time."

"For murder."

I spat.

He stood, said,

"Maybe I will have a drink after all."

He returned with half a bottle of Jameson. Unheard of in any Irish pub unless it was in the wee small hours and you were assured of at least two off-duty cops in the vicinity. He offered to pour for me but I covered my glass with my hand. He took that as the insult it was.

I tried to rein in my racing mind, said,

"As one who has trod the road of revenge and retribution, and was nigh insane with grief afterward

. . . The price was very high and you know what? No peace, either."

He sank a shot, did another but it didn't seem to do much, not even color his cheeks, then placed the glass carefully on the edge of the table, said in a very measured tone, as if he was controlling his temper more than a fear of slurring,

"Appreciate the little lecture on morals but you know what? You hold the twisted broken limbs of your gorgeous child, who has been ravaged in every possible way. The coroner said they placed objects in every . . ."

He faltered.

Looked away.

"In every orifice."

Jesus.

I tried to ease some understanding into my words but like, what the hell, I said,

"I can't get your absolute pain but neither can I be part of this."

He mulled that over, then,

"Would you go and see the Yank who is overseeing the operation?"

"What possible good would that do?"

His body shook and he grimaced.

"Good? Who's talking about fucking *good*? That went into the river with my daughter. I'm asking you for a bit of damn leeway, and don't sweat — I'll pay you for your time."

More to ease him down than acquiesce, I said okay. He wrote down an address, said,

"The gentleman has offices here."

Then he reached into his jacket, passed over a fat envelope, said,

"For your trouble."

I looked at it, asked,

"You had the money ready? You knew I'd agree?"

He stood up, said,

"I'm an accountant; I know exactly what money can buy."

I tried for world-weary, snapped,

"Everyone can be bought, eh?"

He was already leaving, said,

"No, just the empty ones."

I stayed on for another pint after he left, the fat money envelope before me. Tried to tell myself that money has no feeling. You get it, you keep it.

M . . . m . . . m.

Decided I could go see the Yank and just play it as it presented. Thus unsettled, and with a tiny cloud of, if not unknowing, then certainly vague dread trailing.

I wasn't striving to win.

Just wanted to mix up failure a bit.

Told myself I'd take the dog for a long walk, let the ocean blow away whatever ghosts were forming. Soon as I got to my door, I sensed something off. And could hear muted sounds from within. Bracing myself, I pushed it open. The dog ran to greet me, wild love as if he hadn't seen me for a year.

Sitting in my armchair was a woman, dressed like Annie Hall, smoking a thin cheroot. I kid thee fucking not.

Emily.

I said,

"Jesus wept."

She gave that radiant smile, asked,

"Miss me, Jack?"

Already I was off balance, which is what I'd always been with her. No matter what tack I took, she was always out of left field. All you could do was hope the damage would be short. I said,

"See you made yourself at home."

She shook the glass in her hand, said,

"I'm about ready for a refill."

The dog gave me a delighted greeting then, the treacherous bastard, bounded onto her lap. She asked,

"What did you name him?"

I grabbed the bottle from the table, poured one, and refreshed hers. I said,

"Storm."

She rubbed his ears, then,

"How very you."

"Is there any point in asking you where the hell you've been?"

She seemed to be seriously weighing her response, then,

"First I have to choose an accent, add a little drama."

I sighed, almost the way my mother did, her whole wretched life. Said,

"I suppose the truth would be too far a reach?"

She finished her drink, smiled, more to herself than the world, asked,

"But where's the fun in that?"

The Annie Hall persona was already evaporating and a new hard force sliding in. She said,

"I worked for a hedge fund in New York; everyone should learn how to steal professionally."

Ah, fuck.

I said,

"The banks here found it came naturally."

A sharp tone.

"Don't interrupt, Taylor."

The dog gave her a look, like,

"Seriously?"

"I married a dude in Vegas and, believe me, that was plain tacky."

She was beginning to sound a lot like Sinead O'Connor and that not even I could stomach. I waited.

"Then I took a holiday on Turks and Caicos, see how the superrich play. Guess what?"

"Bored the arse off you."

And she laughed, genuinely, though with her, the term *genuine* was a tad misleading. She nigh sang,

"Exactly. No wonder I missed you. You're so . . . hmm . . . sharp, for your age."

She had the Irish knack of simultaneously patting your head and putting her shoe in your arse. I asked,

"And what, dare one inquire, are your plans now?"

She reached into her bag, a tote that had the logo

. . . *not friggin' Gucci!*

Cute.

Took out a gold cigarette case, extracted what appeared to be a Virginia Slim. I recognized the distinctive motif and, God forgive me, could even remember the slogan back in the day. I can't bring meself to repeat it, it's too folksy, and, fuckit, I can't do folksy.

She lit it with a simple Bic, a girl with all the commercial contradictions. She inhaled like a redneck, all corpse-sucked-in-cheeks, then exhaled, got into lecture mode. Began,

"Jacky, our last adventure, adventures? Think of it like a TV pilot. Especially as you've such a hard-on for U.S. drama. Well, the good news is we've been picked up for a second season and hey, I'm not promising Golden Globes but we're in the game."

I reached for the cig case, and took out what appeared to be your basic cigarette, without a slogan, lit up, said,

"Staying with your analogy, I've decided to go solo, focus on my own series."

If I had hoped to amuse her, I was wrong.

Very.

She near spat.

"Cunt, you are under contract."

Even the dog moved under the chair at the vehemence; he'd been reared on aggression. I kept the steel out of my tone, said,

"Endgame, lady, time to fold the crazy tent and bring the bazaar to further shores."

She was on her feet, all five-foot-four of her, all of it mad as a loon. She snarled,

"I know where the bodies are buried. The nails? Remember them, that they took out of my dear dad and the asshole who killed your dog?"

This was literally the whole summary of my last horrendous case. I took a breath, said,

"You drop a dime on me, bitch, you go down too."

And she laughed, said,

"You dumb Mick — down is where I live."

Before I could reply to this, she reached into the bag again, pulled out a package, said,

"Got you a present, homey."

Fuck.

Hard to flow with her changes. The dog, seeing the package, was all ears, maybe he'd score. I took the present, said,

"Thank you."

And got the radiant smile. Then,

"Well, come on, boss, open up that sucker."

I held it up to my ear, listening for ticking. Pulled the paper off and there was a fancy box, containing a watch, Patek Philippe. I was lost for an answer, I mean, the usual shite, like,

"Gee, you shouldn't have."

Always sounded so awful, but I had nothing else. She was amused at my dilemma, said,

"Not used to kindness, yeah?"

I tried,

"It is just . . . so much!"

She was gathering her stuff, preparing to leave, nudged the dog's ears, asked,

"How'd you know it's not a knockoff?"

"I dunno, you seem like the real deal sometimes."

That seemed to trigger a memory and she zoned for a moment then snapped back, said in a harsh tone,

"Whoa, Jack, beneath the shallow surface is . . . ice."

Then in an effort to rein in, added,

"Anyway, as they say in the soaps, you will always have a little bit of time for me."

Lot of ways I could go on this but I took,

"Supposing it's real, real time that is."

Intrigued her, asked,

"If it's not?"

"Then I'm back to my usual act, faking it."

"I'm afraid of people who are afraid
of dogs." (Anonymous)

The Grammarian fucked up. After, he'd think,

"Who let the dogs out?"

He had heard a man use and abuse the language in a way that seemed to proclaim,

"I'm freaking ignorant and proud of it."

Uh-oh, no way.

He'd tracked the guy back to his home off Devon Park. Nice quiet residential area and no neighborhood watch. Perfect. The guy had gone in his front door so he went round the back. Small garden, good. He checked he had the letter, a vowel, ready then began to make his way up the path and fuck.

A dog.

Big.

And in the lunge, narrowly missed G's face. But undeterred, the dog swirled, fast, ready for another try. G picked up a water bucket and let rip. Knocked the dog back as the back door opened and the man, screaming,

"Was you want, I'll kick your arse"

G scrambled back over the fence and ran for his life, thinking

"... Was you want?"

What on earth kind of language was that?

"The thing is, if you just do stuff and nothing happens, what's it all mean? What's the point?"
(Jesse Pinkman, in *Breaking Bad*)

The accountant who had asked me to look into the death of his daughter. I checked him out. He was serious money. Had all the heavy accounts in the city and beyond. A little more checking and discovered he had served as an officer with the UN so his saying he had *friends* who would *help* him was definitely a sign he had been telling the truth. The company that employed his daughter and was responsible for her death, Real Time Inc., was situated close to the docks. Brand-new state-of-the-art building, so lots of cash. The managing director was Brad Clear, which told me exactly nothing. Had an MBA in business from some midwestern college.

I thought,

"Okay, let's go pay Brad a visit."

I wore my Garda coat, still being demanded back by the Department of Justice. Despite the recent firing/resignation of the minister of justice over Garda whistle-blowing, it seemed my coat was still a vital necessity to them. No wonder they were fucked. I had a crisp new white shirt, bespoke in Jermyn Street, or so the collar claimed, and cost me five euros in the charity shop. Black 501s and Doc Martens, street scuffed. Ran my fingers through my hair to give that overall look of an eccentric writer or someone who could give a careless fuck. I had the news on and aw, damn it, Joan Rivers died. A true loss, so few left who actually said the things most of us were afraid to even think. And she pissed on PC. How could you not applaud that, when people were so afraid of offending somebody with any opinion they nervously aired? She had brought not so much joy as a wicked glee in taking down celebrities and other riffraff.

I walked down Shop Street and the papers were telling us that some economic recovery was already apparent. But to whom? And promising us that the coming budget wouldn't be so harsh. Just bullshit cover for the water charges due at the end of October. Despite the glut of scandals of fat cats stealing from the very charities they headed, there were still gangs of collectors on the street. And I mean gangs, no longer the lone supplicant, but groups, lest they be confronted.

A busker was massacring "Knockin' on Heaven's Door" and a tap dancer was only halfheartedly going through the motions. Two teenagers accosted me demanding I support some camogie team. I said,

"Gimme a break."

I was sorely tempted to nip into Garavan's for a fast Jay but figured I'd soldier on. Top of Quay Street, I looked down to see straggling hen parties looking as if they had been doused in disappointment. Two young tourists checked me out, decided I was reasonably normal, which in Shop Street is some feat these days, and asked if I might know where they would find the *craic*.

I hadn't the heart to tell them that since the new government decided to tax us into oblivion, the word had more or less lost all meaning. I told them to check out Naughton's pub. Pushing, they went,

"But is there music?"

I pointed down the street, said,

"There's all kinds of tunes but I can't vouch for any melody."

I got to the docks as the sun made a late appearance. Glanced up at what was almost a blue sky, took a deep breath, and entered the office of Real Time Inc. An all-biz secretary/receptionist asked if I had an appointment. I said,

"No, but Mr. Clear will be glad to see me, I bring tidings of investigation."

Lest I be IRS or worse, she picked up a phone, did some whispering, then said,

"Down the corridor, first on the right."

I gave her my best smile but it didn't seem to bring any sun into her sky. Brad Clear was one big guy, over six feet, looked like someone who'd played in the NFL but some time ago. He had one of those stomachs that seems to have a life of its very own. And as always, he emphasized it with the tightest shirt. A very expensive suit did absolutely nothing to hide the gut, nor did he seem to care. He was maybe in that indefinable good for sixty-five or terrible for fifty age bracket. What remained of his blond hair was long at the back and, I prayed, not in one of those god-awful ponytails.

The face though: a study in opposites, what they call a generous mouth below a nose that veered to the left and the hardest dark eyes I have even encountered. The utter kill-all-the-hostages hue. Something else, too, a spark of malignancy and black amusement. He came from behind a massive desk, of course, with his hand extended, said in a good ole boy roar,

"Brad Clear, and you are?"

"Jack Taylor."

He smiled, a dark and vicious thing, said,

"Tell yah, buddy, that don't mean Jack shit to me."

In that good ole tone.

I took back my almost crushed hand, my mutilated fingers already acting out, said,

"Tom Shea, the accountant, asked me to look into the death of his daughter."

He stared at me, asked,

"Is that meant to clarify something?"

Now I got to smile, said,

"Thing is, she took part in some of your training videos."

He stayed with the *Gee, shucks, buddy, you darn lost me there* act. I reached into my jacket, took out the photos of the girl, the postmortem ones, laid them on the desk, said,

"See if this jogs your memory."

He reeled back in mock horror, said,

"That there is some real ugly shit, partner."

52

You see truly shocking pictures and the range of reactions runs the gamut of

Shock

Through

Revulsion

To

Disbelief.

He wasn't even in the neighborhood of giving a toss. I had gone there as a vague way of earning some of the accountant's money and that would be it, in, out, adios. But this prick's attitude changed all that. Before I could answer, he said,

"Fellah, I see so many chicks on any given day, it's like a turkey shoot."

I stared at him. Could he have chosen a more inappropriate simile? He moved back behind his desk, then slapped his leg up on the desk, displaying very fancy cowboy boots. I could see the hand stitching, ornate finish from across the room. He said,

"These here boots, made by hand in Airline, Texas. But that don't mean diddly to you, right? My point being, small-time huckster like you, you wouldn't make in a year what I laid out for these babies."

I said,

"You're correct, I don't know a whole lot about the Lone Star State save for Shiner Bock and Maker's Mark, but one of their sayings seems to fit you."

He was digging this, having him a whole swell sweet time, asked,

"Is it what we call a swagger, walking?"

And he was laughing, not the kind of laugh you'd hear from a person who had much of a relationship to humanity but that cackle that seeps from the bottom of something rotten. I said,

"All hat and no cattle."

Snapped him right back, the dark fire in his eyes again. He snapped,

"The fuck are you? You're not the cops, you got any kind of . . . I . . . D?"

Aggression leaking all over his tone. I said,

"I was going to try concerned citizen but that's more your letter to the *Irish Times* gig so let's say I'm the outrider for an expedition force."

This seemed to amuse him and he said,

"Wherever you're heading with this, I don't see it ending in Miller time."

He gave me a long hard look. The true hard cases don't do that; by the time you've got their attention, you're already cold. He said,

"You're some sort of washed-up cop or army, but from the state of your fucked fingers, your whole . . ."

Paused.

"Ensemble, I'd say at best you're a poor excuse for a messenger boy."

He sat down, shrugged, said,

"But you need to fuck off now, I'm tired of you."

I took a slow appraisal of the office, then settled my eyes on him, said,

"Past ten years, I've met a whole array of sick fucks, crazies, killers, your whole tier of the very shite of society but I'll give you this. You are the only one that might make it feel personal again."

I bade a hearty farewell to the frosty receptionist but she didn't even deign to raise her head. There was a huge tropical plant in the corner, I managed with difficulty to raise it and then, with more force than I knew I had, I hurled it at the plate glass window, said,

"Think of it as window dressing."

That evening, I was having some quiet time, had walked the dog, who was now curled on the sofa, snoring lightly, all peaceful in his small world. I was watching Billy Bob Thornton in the TV series *Fargo*. Just wonderful, as good as the movie and that's some claim. An all-time gold gig from Billy Bob. A knock on the door, so light it didn't stir the dog. I was wearing a loose T with the faded logo

"*Black Mask* original."

And worn to a thread 501s. My feet bare. I opened the door to a fast punch in the face, sent me reeling back, followed by two burly guys in dark clothing. The dog was off the couch and a kick flung him across the room. Without a sound, save *Fargo* muted, I got a systematic beating but all I could focus on was, was the dog all right? After a last kick to the face, one of the guys leaned forward, the smell of curry and tobacco on his breath, and hissed,

"Who is all cattle now?"

Would it have ended there? I don't know, but a shout from the doorway of

"I called the Guards."

Had them leave, without any great haste. Almost relaxed. My neighbor had shouted. Now he bent over me, said,

"The ambulance is on its way."

"The dog . . ."

Was okay, if bruised, and his pride hurt that he hadn't been more canine. Went for us both. I passed out then, thinking my toes were cold. I spent a day in the ICU but then was released to a ward. Ridge arrived with a surly guy in plain clothes. She stared at me with anything but sympathy. Said,

"Don't you ever get tired of this shite?"

I managed to move my head, asked,

"No grapes?"

The guy with her put away his notebook, said to her,

"Let's go; he has nothing to tell us."

Ridge gave me a final disgusted look and I asked,

"Don't you want to know who did this?"

Ridge said,

"Before we get to that, are you aware that a company called Real Time Inc. took out a restraining order against you? Apparently there was an incident involving a window?"

I had to hand it to Clear. He had snookered me and then had his goons beat the living shit out of me. Ridge said,

"We're waiting . . . for the people who did this to you."

I closed my eyes, said,

"Person or persons unknown."

Ridge leaned over, right in my battered face, said,

"No more screwing around. You crop up in my sights again, I will have you for obstruction, and just about anything else I can drum up."

After they left, a nurse came and did the fluff-up-the-pillows ritual they seem to do anytime you get comfortable. She said,

"You must be an important fellah having all those Guards visit you."

"Trust me, importance has very little to do with it."

She stood back, hands on hips, asked,

"Are you after getting yourself in a small bit of bother?"

I nearly laughed but the broken ribs advised otherwise. I said,

"Not sure small would quite cover it."

She gave that tolerant humph that Irishwomen are born with, asked,

"How will your wife take this?"

Now I did laugh, pain and all, said,

"She shows up, that might be the biggest beating of all."

She considered that and just as I thought I might have won her over, she flourished,

"Ah, you'd need to get over yourself."

I woke in the middle of the night, desperate for a pee. Managed to get out of bed and struggle down the ward. Outside the bathroom were two patients, trailing IVs and looking for all the world like . . .

They were on sentry?

I asked,

"What's up, guys?"

One of them, a guy named Scanlon, former bus driver, now on permanent disability, like so many of the city's civil servants, said,

"Cig vigil."

What?

"Like you're mourning them?"

He gave a small laugh, moved his IV line like a dancing partner, said,

"See, you can't smoke on the hospital grounds or on any of the businesses across the road, so, what? A guy is going to trail his line half a mile to grab a smoke?"

I could see the logic, asked,

"So can I like, you know, get in?"

He moved aside, shouted,

"Okay, guys, he checks out."

Inside, it was Dante's Seventh Circle. Clouds of smoke. I did my biz, was heading out amid the throng of smokers, when Scanlon appeared out of the mists, asked,

"Wanna drink, Jack?"

I smiled, said,

"Next you'll have a card game going."

Without missing a beat, he said,

"Booth three, five-card stud."

I declined and Scanlon said to me,

"Before I came into hospital, I bought a scratch card."

I waited, this could be . . .

"I won fifty thousand and gee, I'm a little short until I get the money so I was thinking . . ."

Or

"I'm buying a villa in Portugal."

Nope.

Like this:

"I got three stars and sent it to the TV show."

This was supposed to make some sort of sense and true, I do try to keep up with . . . um . . . *popular culture*, but *The X Factor* had eroded any chance of ever making intelligence out of the abyss of stupidity we had reached. He continued,

"Thing is, I got my name called and now I'm due on the show to win the big prize in two weeks."

He sighed, said,

"But I'm on disability, right? So, you think they'd cop if my brother went in my place?"

Jesus, grand criminal enterprise. I asked,

"He willing to do it?"

He gave me the look, like,

"Are you *not* paying attention?"

He said,

"Fuck sakes, Jack, he is as thick as a government backbencher."

Okay.

I'm sure there was some ironic conclusion to this yarn but I was suddenly tired, of the whole damn country and people having to scratch their way to anything resembling a life of dignity.

"The wrath of God is
A fearsome thing
But the wrath of
Ungodliness
Is real and now."
(*The Book of Amy*)

Early next morning, I was awakened by the nurse and two porters. In hospital, everything happens early, especially death. I said to her,

"Kicking me out, I hope."

She gave me that Irish look that translates simply as "Ah, shut up."

She said,

"You're being moved."

Get this —

To a private room.

Yeah, fuck.

When people are being left on trolleys for days on end, and there is barely standing room for most, a private room is unbelievable. They got me up there and when I was settled in the bed, the nurse said, not in admiration but with malice,

"You must have powerful friends."

I said, half meaning it,

"I'll give it to somebody who really needs it."

She considered that, then,

"You might just do that but this hospital runs on paper, administration, and once it's written down, bad or stupid, it gets done."

I asked,

"Would it help if I feel undeserving?"

She nearly smiled, said,

"We agree on that, the undeserving bit."

As I surveyed the spacious room she turned to go, paused, then,

"You know, I'd say, in your day, you were a fine thing."

Okay.

Not wanting to fuck with that, I very nearly shut it, but . . .

But

I asked,

"And now?"

"Now, you know, you're just like old."

Come noon, high or otherwise, a young doctor appeared with the ubiquitous chart. He looked all of sixteen, said,

"Mr. Taylor."

Had that Dublin 4 accent that spoke of privilege and confidence, spoke like Bono and, Christ, who wants that? I said,

"I thought all the young guns had emigrated."

He didn't smile. No, a serious young man with a serious agenda. He said,

"Actually I have a position in Dubai and will be taking that up soon."

Of course.

He read through my chart, said,

"This is not my first rodeo."

Now I smiled, countered,

"*Justified.*"

He knew the show but went with,

"You have been, mmm ... in many incidents, mutilated fingers, broken nose, ribs, injured leg, and, oh, Lord, a hearing aid. Please tell me you work in a library."

"I used to be a cop."

Even now, it hurts, the past tense. I added,

"I'm working on a quieter life."

A hint of a smile. He said,

"Not sure that is working out for you."

Then read some more:

"A problem with alcohol and prescription drugs."

He looked at the morphine button by my side and I went,

"No, don't even think about it."

He said,

"Just don't ... abuse it."

Yeah.

Morphined hours later, I woke from a fluff dream where I was ... happy. Jesus, that dope is mighty. And sitting at the end of my bed was Madonna.

Emily, in Madonna gear, circa 2005, the workout gloves and the wife-beater shirt. She certainly was glowing, if not from exercise, something very fine. She asked,

"How are you liking the room?"

Took me a minute to focus, get some water for my dry mouth, then,

"You got this?"

She held out a bunch of grapes, said,

"Know how many hotshots I had to blow?"

Phew.

I said,

"Thank you, and for the grapes."

She moved closer, did the air kiss, mocking herself as she did so. Said,

"Ain't no free lunch, right?"

I relaxed back in the bed, almost as ready as you can be for whatever insanity would follow. I said,

"Not a whole lot I can achieve from here."

Shrugged that off with,

"Doctors say you are good to go in a few days."

"How come they told you? I mean, bit early for a blow job."

She took a grape, threw it in the air, and bingo, caught it expertly in her mouth, said,

"I'm your daughter."

God forbid.

It was hard to say if she was even pretty. She had the necessary details to add up to that but they'd been arranged just off center. Yet, she had this life force, a sheer constant burst of light, tinged with the darkness, of course, but you were drawn in. I asked,

"So, what am I going to have to do, to, um, earn my keep?"

She gave me a long calculated look, as if she were getting the measurements for a body bag and, in her case, never rule out the crazy, and said,

"There's a guy running round offing folks for bad grammar."

As usual she blended, mixed, and cajoled a number of accents and slang, all of which kept you, if not on edge, at least on your toes. I asked,

"You know this how?"

"A Guard told me."

Sometimes, if the effect was right, she just went with the bald truth. I suddenly wanted a cigarette, no idea why one particular addiction raises its needy head. They just do. I tried,

"Seriously, a guy is killing people for that?"

She gave a mock frown, said,

"Dude has a point. Civilization begins its slide when the language is fucked."

She might well have believed that. Wouldn't be the worst of her notions. I asked,

"This concerns you and now it seems me, how?"

She did a little skip across the floor. Why? God knows. Said,

"I'm a little bored, you know, need a challenge, and you, my sleuth friend, are going to assist me."

I shook my head, said,

"Even the doctor thinks I need to, um, ease off on . . . my active life."

She looked as if she might be considering a headstand as she gauged the distance near my bed, asked,

"Don't you want to know the second favor?"

I didn't.

She said,

"I want to see my mother, and I want you to come with me."

Whoa.

"But you hate your mother."

"Why I want you to come with me so I don't kill her."

I didn't have a whole argument to run here as I had loathed my own mother. She'd been dead a time now but her poison still filtered through most of my existence. She had made my beloved father's life a living hell and when I turned out to be pretty much a total fuckup, she was as delighted as if I'd become a priest. Of course I could have become a priest and killed two birds with one prayer but those are the breaks. She'd done that gig that was popular in the country when we had no economy, fucked or otherwise: she'd gotten herself a tame priest who tagged along and lapped up her pious bullshit.

I had met Emily's mother in the last game and she was a pitiful drunk. One drink from the abyss.

Emily said,

"She got sober."

"Seriously?"

A flash of anger in those lovely eyes, and you got a peek at the steel that she hid behind all the play personas. Emily gathered up her stuff, said,

"Bitch, just when I thought it could only be a matter of weeks until she choked on her own vile vomit, she goes and gets sober; really, really fucking annoying."

I decided to let that dog bark on its own, no gain in my pithy comments further. She paused at the door, said,

"Heal fast, Jack-o. We have a shitload of work to do."

A thought struck her. She asked,
"You still watching *Justified*?"
"Religiously."

"Ignorant people think it's the *noise* which
fighting cats make that is so aggravating,
but it ain't so; it's the sickening grammar they
use." (Mark Twain)

"And it was during that period that I came
across the fundamental rule of academia.
If you don't know it, fake it." (Pete Dexter)

I was discharged from the hospital two days later. The doctor gave me a pep talk, beginning like this,

"A man of your age . . ."

Translates as

"Tops, a year."

He did give me a painkiller prescription, warning,

"These are heavy-duty . . ."

(I should fucking hope so.)

"And I trust you will use discretion and due diligence."

Doctors nowadays speak more like lawyers and lawyers won't speak at all without heavy cash up front. I said,

"Thank you for all your care."

He looked to see if he detected a barb, added,

"And absolutely no alcohol."

"As if I would."

I called a cab from the River Inn, situated right across from the hospital, and they do a roaring trade. The barmaid, Mary, said,

"Jesus, Jack, you look pale."

"But willing. I'll have a Jay and pint."

My timing was good, finished both as the cab pulled up. I left a tip for Mary, who said,

"You're the only guy who does that."

"Due diligence,"

I said.

She shook her head, said,

"I don't know what you mean but then I never do."

The cabdriver was a Man United fan.

Alas.

He started,

"We'd a nice win on Saturday. I think Rooney is going to be a fine captain."

Would I bother?

I would.

Said,

"He got sent off."

He eyed me in the mirror, not seeing much he liked, then,

"Take that fucking Arsenal, beaten in twelve matches by Chelsea."

I had nothing to say to that.

He took my silence as assent, said,

"You hear about that guy is killing people for talking bad?"

I didn't know it was out there, asked,

"How are the people feeling about that?"

He cheered up, could be the voice of the populace if briefly, said,

"They're hoping he'll go after the government."

He then went into a long harangue about the water charges and I said,

"Just drop me here."

As I paid him, he said,

"Don't mind me saying so but you're a bit pale."

Jesus.

When I opened the door to my apartment, I was near knocked down by the pup. Did twirls and turns of delight and in truth I found my heart sing at such a welcome. A moment later, my neighbor appeared, said,

"Good to have you back, Jack."

He had stocked my fridge and even laid in beer, cold and plenty. I tried to pay him but he was having none of it, said,

"Minding that pup is a joy."

I took a sneak look at my neighbor. He was of tremendous help to me in so many ways yet I knew next to nothing about him. Hell, he might even be the Grammarian for all I detected. I gave the pup some chews and a rough ear rub, then fetched two cold ones from the fridge, said,

"Take a pew."

He settled himself in the armchair, took a long swig, then asked,

"Would you have a cigarette?"

I would and did.

Said,

"I didn't know you smoked."

He leaked a smile, said,

"No reason why you should. Just odd times I get the urge and one thing I've learned at my age is, have at some of the urges."

Never having resisted any of my own, was I going to give him an argument?

No.

I asked,

"How are you liking Galway?"

He mulled that over, then,

"I love the poetry of the streets, if that doesn't sound too much of an asshole thing to say."

A moment, then we both laughed. I said,

"Poetry and assholes, our speciality. In fact they are intrinsically linked."

He gave me a very direct look, not something you get much with English people. They tend to come at you sideways. He said,

"You have a great fondness for language."

What could I answer but,

"Like the Grammarian I hear."

He was debating something, then,

"My days in the army, the squad called me Doc."

Was I to call him that?

Continued,

"Not a medical thing but I could doctor any paper you desired."

Wondering where this was headed, I tried,

"You think I need some . . . papers?"

He smiled, and the change, his whole personality altered, he looked . . . um . . . *doctored*? Said,

"Never know when the shit hits the fan and it's time to move fast."

Then he veered away, said,

"I've been reading Paula Fox, *The Western Coast*, and she reminded me of the small subtle damages we inflict on each other."

"Haven't read her."

"She went out of print in 1992 and then Jonathan Franzen bigged her, the mags got hold of her connection to Courtney Love, and, voilà, she's experiencing a mini resurgence."

Was there a moral, an inference? I couldn't join the dots so went lame, said,

"Guess it's never too late to grab the brass ring."

Lame.

He finished his beer, stood, said,

"I'm glad you are home, Jack."

And it sounded as if he meant it. I had that awkward male moment of

"So, okay, do we hug or what the fuck?"

The pup came trailing the lead and saved us. I said,

"Looks like I'm going for a walk."

"He could see her hands holding her bare skull and a teacher-voice in his mind saying this was woman, a hunter. The voice saying look at the fucking teeth on her, this was a man-eater." (Elmore Leonard, *Freaky Deaky*)

I got in touch with a semiretired villain I'd known back when my friend Stewart had been alive. The loss of Stewart weighed heavy, like all the others. Sweeny, the ex-crook, spent most of his time in Spain but had returned. He said,

"Too many Irish drug dealers setting up shop there."

We met in Roldan's, a quiet pub near what had once been thriving docks, now was just a wasteland like the country itself. Sweeny was brown as oak and had more lines than an Ordnance Survey map. His voice was raspy from too many cigarettes but it worked for him, gave him a gravitas that was an asset in his former line of work. He greeted me warmly, if raspily. He said,

"Look like you've been in the wars, Jack."

"I was caught without a hurley."

He liked that. His weapon used to be a solid iron bar. He was drinking wine and had ordered a pint and chaser for me. Knew my form. He nodded at the wine, said,

"Got a taste for it on the Costa."

Drank a sip, then,

"Boring as fuck out there. Us Irish, we don't do sun real well. I got me an iPad and, after a few glasses of this shit, I'd start buying stuff on Amazon. I wanted to see *The Bridge* and guess I was a bit befuddled as I ended up with

. . . get this,

The Bridge, Danish original

The Tunnel . . . Australian

The Bridge, the Yanks setting it on the Rio Grande.

So I'm watching all three on consecutive nights and I get to see the icy blond chick in three different nationalities."

I smiled, asked,

"How'd that work out for you?"

He sighed, said,

"Fuck it. I gave up, went back to *Father Ted*, the devil you know, eh? But you didn't ask to meet me to discuss the merits of European crime drama versus the Yanks."

"No, I wanted to get some armory."

We decided on something light, in terms not of stopping power but of weight. He took off for about half an hour and I listened to the jukebox.

I kid thee not, an actual jukebox with no fucking Rihanna. Blessings. A tune playing:

"If I Didn't Have a Dime."

Oh, Lord.

The days of the dance halls and show bands. When the only booze you brought into the hall was the booze in your belly and priests patrolled outside to ensure there was no impropriety as their colleagues abused the children of the country and destroyed most of a generation.

82

Next tune up was one of the first pop songs that ever registered with me:

"From the Underworld"

By the Herd.

Right, who the fuck is the Herd?

The lead singer left the band. Peter Frampton, who became a global heartthrob. Cover of *Rolling Stone* and all points north. Where was he now?

Hanging with David Cassidy?

Sweeny was back, with the ubiquitous McDonald's bag. In my time, weapons are always delivered thus. Some kind of postmodern statement? Or simply the nearest shit to hand? Sweeny grimaced, asked,

"You wanted fries with that?"

I asked the freight and rough it was. But these days of government levies on everything, from water to pretax scams, it was par for end-times. I asked,

"Take a check?"

Another bright scheme from our leaders.

Yeah, abolish checks. Anything that would make life even more fucking miserable than it was. The juke played

"Dust in the Storm"

Marc Roberts.

Sweeny said,

"That McDonald's? You want to tell me what's going down there?"

Meaning, why are you tooling up?

I would have liked to have his muscle as a backup but the price of doing biz with villains was a debt that kept on giving. I said,

"It may be nothing, just a little insurance."

He didn't buy that but, what the hell, like he could give a fuck? He veered, asked,

"You been hearing about this Grammarian fellah?"

I nodded, then,

"Seems to have the public wind."

He began to gather his stuff, preparing to leave, said,

"Fucking amateur though."

"You think?"

He was on his feet, the light in the bar darkening his Costa tan, said,

"'Course. He left witnesses."

The Glock was a nine-mm, one of the new models with a seventeen-shot capability. Now I just needed seventeen people to shoot. I went to see the accountant whose daughter had been killed. I had the gun in my Garda jacket. Always see your money guys with weight. They piss you off, you have a solid argument.

Made me wait half an hour. I read an old *Reader's Digest* while I waited and increased my word power. Learned that an intransitive verb acts by itself, like a PI in fact.

But without the baggage.

E.g.,

I sleep

I fall

I shoot

Or, if you're Irish,

"Jesus wept."

Finally I got ushered into his impressive office. He didn't seem pleased to see me, opened,

"Look like you have been in the wars."

I explained my visit to his daughter's former employer and the resultant hiding I received. He asked,

"You sure it was connected?"

Was he kidding?

I asked,

"You're kidding, right?"

He was definitely even more unimpressed. Said,

"Your line of work, I would think that beatings are all in a day's fun."

The fuck was this? The guy hired me and now he's going all defensive and good citizen? I said,

"You hired me."

He sighed and,

"Yes, but not to draw attention to yourself. When we take this player off the board, you think we want to leave a trail?"

Jesus wept.

I asked,

"You taking me off the case?"

He stood up so that I might admire the cut of his Armani suit, said,

"We'd been somewhat wrong-footed by some past successes of yours and it seemed that you might, in your stumbling fashion, find out actual evidence but, alas, you have become the very drunken collateral we heard you were."

I said,

"That is atrocious English."

He looked down at his desk, said,

"Good-bye, Mr. Taylor."

I moved to the door, reaching for some exit line if not of dignity, at least of significance, tried,

"For an accountant of some repute, you figured one factor wrong."

He gave me a look of borderline pity, asked,

"Oh, what might that be?"

"Pigheadedness."

Outside, the rain came lashing down and I held my face up to it, hoping . . . what? Any cleansing available to me had been shut off at source so long ago and now, of course, the government was making us pay for any drop of water. I went to Garavan's, ordered,

"A pint, a Jay, and no conversation."

They came in exactly that order.

As I reached for my wallet, my hand touched the butt of the Glock and I derived that scant comfort it gave. I stayed for over an hour and when I readied to leave, the bar guy shouted,

"Nice chatting to you, Jack."

Friday morning, Emily picked me up at my apartment. She was driving a red Kia, which, if it was a statement, said,

"I'm dafter than you thought."

I got in and she pointed out a Starbucks container on the dash, said,

"Wasn't sure how you like it so I had them pile in everything."

Which might well have been true. I asked,

"When did Starbucks open in Galway?"

She gave me the look that urged,

"Get with the bloody game."

Said,

"They have an outlet in the college."

"So they figure the ordinary folk don't drink coffee?"

"No, they know that students will drink any old shit."

I tried,

"You know they don't pay any tax, Starbucks?"

She shrugged. Not easy when you're maneuvering around the Headford road, said,

"Neither do you."

I could have asked how she knew so much about my affairs but it opened up an area that was best left alone. I asked,

"Does your mum know we're coming?"

She scoffed, mimicked,

"Mum . . . She's a cunt."

Killing the whole thread of that. I found the radio dial, and got Galway Bay FM, *The Big Breakfast Show*. He was playing the White Stripes. Listened to that for a bit then. We were coming up to Shop Street and my eyes spotted Whelans Pharmacy. I said,

"The owner of that pharmacy, Michael, sat beside me in school."

She scoffed,

"And you? What, just decided to be a failure as your school friend made a career?"

Jesus.

So much for sharing.

I went another tack, tried,

"When you were . . . away . . . where exactly were you?"

She mused over that, then,

"I was amassing money."

"For what?"

She waved her hand vaguely, said,

"Money isn't always protection but it sure makes a basis for attack."

Riddle me that.

We'd arrived at her mother's house. Before, when I had visited, it had been a shroud of darkness, everything dying. Now it was renewal in neon. Brightly painted and, even I noticed, new curtains. It looked . . . welcoming?

Emily warned,

"Follow my lead, you hear?"

Jesus.

I asked,

"Like good cop bad cop?"

She gave me the look, sneered,

"Like in, you say fuck all."

I could do that.

The door was opened by a woman who looked healthy and alive, no trace of the wretched drunk I had encountered last time. She gave a small smile and began to open her arms but Emily brushed her aside, saying,

"A hug? Really?"

Guess not.

I stood there, saying, you guessed it, fuck all. Her mother said,

"Would you like to come in, Mr . . . ?"

"Jack, Jack Taylor."

No memory of our previous time or the gallon of whiskey I had fed her. Inside, the house was a testament of OCD. Spotless and solitary. She offered,

"Some tea, coffee? I'm afraid we don't have any . . . beverages."

Emily laughed, an unpleasant sound, said,

"Being as you drank it all and more."

We stood in the grim aftermath of that for a minute until Emily broke the tableau, said,

"You dragged us all the way out here. What's the big deal?"

Her mother looked beseechingly at me and I moved to go outside but Emily shot me a look. Her mother said,

"I wanted to make amends to you."

Emily laughed out loud, spat,

"How will you do that? Restore my virginity that Daddy took?"

Phew.

Fuck it. I got the hell out of there. I could hear shouting behind me and started to walk down the road. An articulated lorry came hugely along and more in desperation than seriousness I put out my thumb and . . . he stopped.

With my bad leg took me a time to climb up there. Settled in the massive cab and said,

"Thanks a lot."

The Polish driver said,

"Random acts of kindness."

Alas, his good deed was fouled by a tape of Black Sabbath. You have not known damnation until you hurl along the motorway, Sabbath roaring in your ears, and a driver eating a thick bagel laden with dripping mayo and tomatoes.

It did save chat so there's that. He dropped me off at Eyre Square. A wag I knew from Garavan's watched me climb down, asked,

"New job, Taylor?"

I said,

"With the water charges, we all have to improvise."

I sat on a bench until a guy approached and sold me a sheet of Xanax. Not exactly the stuff they dealt on *The Wire* but it does the job. He took the money, said,

"You ever need anything else, here's my number."

Might be my imagination but he looked a little like Ozzy Osbourne.

"Never judge a dog's pedigree by the kind of books he does not chew." (Irish logic)

The Grammarian

Oliver Parker Wilson. Now that's a name. To conjure with. In Galway in the late '50s, there had been two Protestant families. Two! Count 'em. The Hunters, who manufactured prams, and the Wilsons, who were in exports and simply rich. As Protestant they were, of course, apart and almost like suspicious royalty. Money and Protestant, rarities in a poor town. The Hunters were almost popular in that there was no ill feeling toward them and they did bring employment. The Wilsons were just aloof.

Oliver was the only son and sent to Eton. Where he was schooled in barbarism and grammar. Never fully recovered. He took a first at Cambridge and his first breakdown. He believed words were communicating some special meaning only to him. He was uncomfortable, not with being mad, just with people knowing it, so he began to disguise it with an icy politeness. Then softened that with an ironic wit.

Mostly, he felt an overwhelming anger and did what you do with that — he joined the army. Did well until he shot an NCO and, with family influence, was invalided out. And what to do with the lunatic? Trained as a teacher, always a fine route for madness. During a class for O-level English, grammar began to speak to him again, its rules and structures singing a dark song of transcendence. A pupil mangling intransitive verbs drove him to rage he could barely contain. Found that drowning the pupil brought an ease he'd never known.

And

The knowledge that secrecy was his ally. Cover your tracks. Oddly, he had a small circle of friends, ex-army, and fucked up in other ways. They saw his obsession with language as a hoot.

Indeed.

They called him Park. He began to see himself as Park, an eccentric fellow who was essentially harmless as long as you didn't disrespect English. And well he may have continued in this low-level field of carnage, not calling attention to himself but dealing with barbarians discreetly.

Until

A colleague at work exclaimed,

"Texting may well replace common usage."

The sacrilege.

And without due consideration, he had flown at the man. Lost his job and was lucky to escape jail. So, head home. Whoever said you can't go home again didn't come from money. You have money, you can go home any fucking time you like.

He did.

Just in time to bury his elderly parents and take over the large house at the back of the golf links. The city had moved on in his absence: had been rich then back to poor again. But being English was no longer a cachet or a problem. So many nationalities now that the St. Patrick's Day parade was embroiled in rows as to what ethnic group should lead the damn thing. One thing sure: it wasn't going to be anybody Irish.

Park was now aging, but insanity has its perks. A life without regret keeps you young. He had all his hair, his teeth, and a nervous system attuned to chaos that kept him slender. He dressed in the Anglo fashion of tweeds and Barbour. He would have kept dogs save they instinctively ran a mile from him.

Otherwise, he was pretty much the country gent temporarily in the city. Best of all, he played golf. You want to be accepted by the shakers, play golf. You don't even have to be very good. Long as you aren't caught cheating. He had once played with Superintendent Clancy, thus having a solid connection to law enforcement.

Clancy liked to think he was mixing with the aristocracy. If he could just get to meet Bill Clinton, hell, he could run for president.

Park, in his time in mental hospitals, had received shock treatment and found it . . . get this . . . refreshing. Wiped the slate clean and, as he came out of it, he could start all over again, hating the abuse of language. Through trial and mostly error, he had managed to set up his own do-it-yourself electric current treatment. Had more than a few close calls but now he could hook up the cables, put the rubber wedge between his teeth, set the timer, and shock the living shit out of his system.

It accounted for the long falloff between kills. Take out a few language abusers, then shock city and he was almost a model citizen for a few months. Back to the golf links and he was as good a citizen as you could hope to meet, long as you minded your language.

Park

Post

ECT

Passage.

When the power surged through Park, his whole body shook, the rubber retainer dropped from his mouth, and as the power automatically shut off, he slipped to the floor, convulsing slightly. A few more shudders, then he was still, drool leaking from his mouth.

His mind . . .

Careering down a completely blank space, a wind howling in his ears, then a pause as roads of utter whiteness began to form. Cascades of letters began to rain down and he opened his mouth as if he could swallow them. The scene metamorphosed to a wood, his father, and a group of men with shotguns and rifles, repeatedly firing and bringing down pheasant, more than they could ever use. A taste of cordite in his mouth, then his father attempting to force the gun into his small hands, shouting at him, "Be a man, kill them."

No need for Psychology I to figure the impact that would have on a sensitive boy. More shooting, carnage, and a

96

mound of brightly torn bodies as the pheasant were piled up. The boy hugging himself, incanting

A

E

I

O

U

His mother, in the distance, always distant and whispering gently,

. . . Park, darling, never forget the beauty of language, and his father at the long dinner table, pieces of bird hanging from his mouth, shouting,

. . . If you can't speak properly, you should lie with the carcasses. Then flash-forward to Kosovo; a nominal mission with the UN; and moving down a street, snipers taking off the stragglers, fear in his mouth, and the medic saying,

. . . We need morphine.

On a small table near his DIY kit, a bottle of gin (Beefeater), a bucket (silver) of ice, and a neatly thin-sliced lemon stood in readiness. A large hand-painted sign warned,

. . . Do not drink.

Park poured a large Galway crystal tumbler of gin with ice and lemon, drank slowly but with deep appreciation. His mouth was so dry from the procedure.

Whoa . . .

. . . He's drinking? Did the sign not say . . . ?

Of course he drank, he's bat-shit crazy.

"Dogs are very wise. When they are hurt, they slink off to a hiding place and wait until they are recovered before returning." (Agatha Christie)

Park felt the gin course through his system like wildfire and this set off in his head the epic sea battle in *Game of Thrones*, where wildfire is used to destroy the attacking fleet. He bit down, could feel the flames, then physically shook himself as he tried to rearrange what personality remained after the voltage.

He had but a very vague idea of who he was or even where he was. But this was part of the rush, the whole *Stranger in a Strange Land* gig. He had showered, clothed, and generally readied himself before he shocked the shit out of his head.

Now he stood before a full-length mirror and marveled at the nigh-on total stranger who peered back. He said,

"Pleased to meet you, hope you guessed my name."

A wave of dizziness washed over him and he tottered to a chair, thinking,

"Whoosh, this is a blast, whatever the fuck it is."

Interestingly, he cursed only when his mind was at half-mast.

"A question in the form of a statement, known as an embedded question, doesn't require a question mark. The question whether children learn enough grammar remains to be answered."

Park dressed in the Anglo fashion, as if clothes were an afterthought and really should be left to servants. He wore a pair of heavy tan cords, a shirt actually made in Jermyn Street, brogues made in Milan, and a heavy waistcoat made on the Aran Islands. He was about to reach for his wax coat when

. . . the doorbell rang.

"A storm sometimes washes everything clean but mainly just disguises the damage already done." (Emily/Emerald)

I opened the door to a wild welcome from the pup; he did that singsong howl, his whole body straight and his head back. It signaled total happiness. A concept almost totally alien to me though I was around long enough to recognize it. I fixed him his dinner and he fixed his gaze on me, lest I leave in mid-chow. He wouldn't eat if I left the room.

While he ate, I watched David Foster Wallace's *This Is Water* on YouTube. Not sure what it did for me but it got my mind kick-started. The Davids in my viewing life:

David Mamet
David Simon
David Chase
David Milch.

The last I shared a wild streak of drugs, booze, and insanity with.

A knock on the door: my neighbor whom I now addressed as Doc. He seemed to go for it. He came in, rubbed the pup behind the ears, and took a seat. He was carrying a bright-colored box, said,

"I know you pretty much don't get science fiction."

True.

I said,

"I have a hard enough time with plain old reality."

He nodded, then,

"You rate

Breaking Bad

The Wire

Justified

Mad Men

The Sopranos

As among the finest writing today. Am I right?"

"Yeah, pretty much. I think *The Wire* is the great American novel."

He smiled at that.

He handed over the box, said,

"Give this a shot."

I read the title, *Battlestar Galactica*, all twenty-five discs! Went,

"Lord, I'd need another lifetime to commit to this."

As I laid it aside, he said,

"It's got Edward James Olmos and Mary McDonnell."

I was thinking,

". . . Maybe look it up online, then wing that I watched it."

Doc gave one last boost,

"Some critics regard it as maybe the best TV ever made."

I'd take this as science fiction, said,

"And they say *The Big Bang Theory* is funny."

He conceded, asked,

"Any progress in your case, the girl who was murdered?"

I shook my head, my lack of anything on this was embarrassing. I said,

"I'm at that point where I have nothing to go on."

He moved to go, said,

"Treat it a little like life."

"How does that work?"

Very sly smile, then,

"Like an infinite jest."

Park

and

Recreation.

Park stood frozen as the doorbell shrilled again. After his ECT, he would usually wander around the garden in a semi-relaxed daze. Dealing with the world was never on the list. Took him a moment to even recognize what the ring was. Then he moved slowly to answer.

Two

Students.

Collecting for Rag Week.

Boy and girl.

They let the girl do the spiel. She began,

"Dreadfully sorry to inconvenience you, sir, but we are collecting for Rag Week."

She giggled.

"Even though Rag Week is no longer officially recognized, we like to organize some charity events for the homeless."

The boy was smirking, stared amused at the silent Park. He thought,

"Old fellah is out of it."

Park focused on the girl, said,

"I very much doubt you are."

She looked at the boy, like, *hello*, did she miss, like, something? Park's mind wandered for a moment amid a jungle of vowels, then he re-clicked, said,

"Dreadfully. You said you are dreadfully sorry but that is just simply misuse of an adjective. And . . ."

He had to think for a moment, then,

"There is really no call for that."

The girl was going to give some cheek but then went,

"Anyways, you want to give a donation to help the homeless?"

Park debated punching her in the face but it would require more energy that he could expend. He said,

"How could you possibly care for the homeless when you don't care for the rudiments of language?"

Slammed the door in her face.

The girl, named Kiera, one of the generation who had left Irish names like

Mary

Siobhan

Maura

Back with the notion of Mass on a Sunday,

Looked back at Park's house, something tickling at the edge of her consciousness.

The boy, whose interest ranged no further than *The Big Bang Theory*, was, in his mind, a surfer dude/stoner on some beach in

Daytona.

Like he knew Daytona from a hole in his Red Bulled brain. Kiera said,

"Dude, something off back there."

The boy went,

"Duh."

She racked her brain for something she'd been hearing around the town, had a moment, then said to the boy,

"He seemed a bit hung up on language."

The boy was already trying to decide on thick or thin crust from Domino's.

She reached the answer, said,

"Holy shite, the grammar guy."

She took out her phone, checked a number, waited, then said,

"I need to talk to a detective about the dude who's been offing people."

The young Guard thought she was speaking to an American but was clued enough to shout for Ridge, said,

"You need to take this."

"Nothing screams faith in God
Like three inches
Of bulletproof glass
Between the pope
And his flock."

"My life has become being stuck between
A Kindle
And
A bookcase."
(Jack Taylor)

I was listening to Jimmy Norman. He had just received his master's in business and continued to do his radio show.

Impressive.

Ebola was increasingly on a par with the generated paranoia, so any flight from West Africa was close to being shot down. The only light humor in this was Sarah Palin urging Obama to invade Ebola.

The pup was avoiding me as he strongly suspected it was wash day. His own paranoia at play. The local news featured a serious fire on Dockland and loss of life was feared. I wasn't paying full attention. Had been reading David Foster Wallace's first novel,

The Broom of the System

And had to smile at his own dismissal of it as

. . . in many ways it was a

Fuck-off

Enterprise.

You had to love a guy who said that.

"My dog is usually pleased with what
I do because
She is not infected
With the concept
Of what I
Should
Be doing."
(Lonzo Idolswine)

"It seems perverse to insist on using a
capital C for New England Cheddar on
the basis that the cheese is named after
a place in Somerset, England."
(Caroline Taggart, *My Grammar and I
(Or Should That Be "Me"?):
Old-School Ways to Sharpen Your English)*

I was having breakfast in the GBC, the neon nightmare.

Two fried eggs

Fat heartaches sausages

Fried tomatoes (at the green café)

Fried mushrooms

Black pudding

Kidding about the last one

Pot of scalding tea.

You can't, just can't, have coffee with a fry-up.

Halfway through this feast, a shadow fell over me. Looked up.

Emily.

Pissed, in the American sense, launched,

"What did I tell you, eh? Follow my lead, what was not to understand about that?"

I put my fork down. It's impolite to point with it, never mind sticking it in her fucking eyes. I said, quietly,

"F-u-c-k off."

Worked.

She went docile, said,

"If I could just sit a moment."

She reached into her bag, took out an e-cig, and I spotted a book, part of the title, about grammar, by

Sally Wallace.

WTF?

Sally Wallace, mother of David Foster?

No way.

I went,

"Why are you reading about grammar?"

She was still staring at the remnants of my breakfast in a sort of fascinated horror. She said,

"If we're going to catch the Grammarian we need to know about motivation."

Jesus.

I asked,

"The fuck is with the *we?*"

Her eyes took on that hard hue, she hissed,

"You owe me, buster."

Ah, fuck, she was just plain flat-out nuts but she wasn't finished, said,

"Besides, I'm writing a mystery novel."

Well, why not, if every literary hack was taking time out from the *serious vocation of literature and slumming in genre,* she would be just one more opportunist. I said,

"Crime."

"Excuse me?"

In that sharp edgy interrogatory tone we'd imported from American sitcoms. I said,

"This is Europe, we call the genre *crime.*"

Would she concede, would she fuck?

Said,

"The mystery is why the hell I'm bothering to tell you, fellah."

Whack-o.

Easing up, I tried,

"You got a title?"

Big satisfied smile.

No
   One
        Weeps
            on
                Sesame
                    Street.

"Catchy,"

I said.

She seemed pleased with that, and then,

"I'm going to write a *crime* novel channeling David Foster Wallace, blend in the rules of grammar, have a broken-down PI, an enigmatic femme fatale, and oh, for the punters, a lovable scamp, as in the dog, not the PI."

I smiled with no feeling of amusement, said,

"You really love to mind-fuck."

She shook the e-cig as if that would miraculously provide the needed hit, said,

"Not just the mind."

Before I could counter that, a man came bustling in, walked rapidly to the table, extended his hand, said,

"You did it, big man. Didn't think you had it in you."

It was Tom Shea, who had recently fired me from the investigation into his daughter's death, and he seemed genuinely delighted. I asked,

"What are you talking about?"

He gave Emily a quizzical look, asking,

"Can we speak in front of her?"

Emily said,

"I'm his lover."

Took him . . . and me . . . aback.

She smiled, added,

"In truth I'm his trophy wife. We have a love lust gig going. He loves me and I do the lust bit."

He took a moment to rally, then,

"I thought you were a deadbeat, Jack, and then you take out the whole office on the docks, and the American bollix is in there."

The fire I'd heard about on the docks, Jesus.

I said,

"Good grief, I didn't do that."

He winked, fucking winked, said,

"Smart.

Deny

Deny

Deny."

I'm on that page.

"Needless to say, if the Guards ask, I can provide an alibi for you and there will be a sweet bonus in the mail. Payback is a lovely bitch."

And he was gone.

I tried to get my mind around the office being burned and, worse, a man dead. I looked at Emily, said,

"I swear on my father's grave . . ."

She held up a hand, said,

"I know you didn't do it."

I felt a giddy relief, stammered,

"Thanks. Thanks for believing in me."

She gave a harsh laugh, said,

"Idiot, it's not that I believe in you. It's more that I set the fire."

"Dogs come into our lives to teach us about love, they depart to teach us about loss. A new dog never replaces an old dog; it merely expands the heart. If you have loved many dogs, your heart is very big." (Erica Jong)

Back in the '70s, I was stationed briefly in Dublin. I can still remember the first guy I saw wearing bell-bottom pants. Drugs were just becoming part of the culture and dopeheads were beginning to appear and get busted. Our directive was crystal clear.

Guys with long hair, fuck 'em.

And we did, with feeling.

Those months gave me a sense of the street that has saved me many times. I was fit from playing hurling and full of piss and vim. Drinking wild but then so was everybody else. Least anyone I knew. There was a legendary drug cop named Lugs Brannigan, out and about in the '60s, he was the sort of man that Gene Hackman was born to play. October 2014, the first ever bio of him was published. He used his fists to settle most disputes and nobody seemed to think it was worth noting, but he got the job done. He never used a baton, opting for a pair of heavy black gloves, and would lash thugs across the face. This not only got their full attention but had the invaluable ingredient of shame.

Reprimanded once by a judge for his methods, he answered,

"Nothing like a belt in the mouth to stop their actions."

The powers that be kept him to never more than sergeant rank. He had the best approval though. On his retirement, the working girls of Dublin gave him a set of Waterford crystal to say thank you for his protection from abusive men.

I was seeing a girl from Athlone named Rita Lyndsey. Her father was a fire chief so we were somewhat in the same territory. She had a head of gorgeous dark brown curls and I think I was well smitten. She loved to dance, I loved to drink and, when I drank, I could, um, like dancing.

The primo duty in those days was security for visiting rock bands and phew-oh, we got some heavy numbers in those days. Led Zep, the Stones, and even a flying visit from Black Sabbath. As a Guard, I was meant to listen to

Show bands

Country and western.

A duty on a concert by Taste introduced me to Rory Gallagher, and shortly afterward I caught Skid Row, the band that fired Phil Lynott. Gave me a lifelong admiration for guitar heroes. The last few years, I went on a binge of curiosity about what happened to all these guys and I read

Nick Kent

Nina Antonia

Mick Wall

Robert Greenslade

Philip Norman

130

For some weird unconnected reason, all this fire ran through my mind as I tried to grapple with Emily being the arsonist. Close to babbling,

I said,

"I don't know which is worse: that you did it or that you didn't and are claiming it."

She said simply,

"They beat you up, I got payback."

I tried,

"But a man is dead."

She smiled, chilling in its simplicity, said,

"He was a piece of shit."

"It's better to spend money like there's no tomorrow than to spend tonight like there's no money." (P. J. O'Rourke)

Park heard the doorbell sound again and now it had that impatient shrill. His mind was still in the white zone, letters tumbling around like confetti. He felt weightless and yet strung out. He opened the door.

A woman in a dark coat and a tall Guard behind her. Beyond her, he could see Garda vans and cars. He thought,

"Uh-oh."

The woman flashed a warrant card and a formal-appearing sheet of paper. She barked,

"I'm Sergeant Ridge, and this here is a warrant to search your home. You are Parker Wilson, I presume?"

Park found all kinds of wrong in the way she formulated the statement and question. It was in the wrong order.

He asked,

"Shouldn't you at least attempt civility?"

Then his mind flipped and he lunged at her, but halfheartedly. The ECT had weakened him so it was, at best, a feeble effort but sufficient for the tall Guard to push her aside and tackle Park, bring him down heavily with a severe blow to the back of the head. Add this to the gin and the shock treatment and Park was out.

Ridge muttered,

"Jesus."

Guards were running toward the house and she got control, ordered,

"Get him in the van, and search this house top to bottom."

She looked down at the limp form of Park. The Guard asked,

"Is it him, do you think?"

Ridge felt that tingle of greatness hovering, the opportunity to score big. She took a breath, managed a smile, said,

"He is certainly now a person of interest."

The Guard, a recent convert to U.S. idiom, said,

"Fucking A, sister."

"Complete sentences need a subject and a verb. Without these, they are known as fragments."

A storm had been threatening the city for weeks. The government focused on this to lure us away from the horrors of the water charges but it wasn't working. Large-scale marches of ordinary, decent people were increasing and the ministers scoffed. The leader of the Labour Party had been especially condescending about the protesters until

She was trapped in her car by them for over two hours.

Ebola continued to wreak havoc in Africa. Of course what do the powers that be do when they want to distract the public? Fall back on the old reliable scare:

. . . Bird flu.

Yeah, time to float that handy threat again.

In the European qualifiers after a wonderful draw with the world champion, Germany, we were beaten by a newly invigorated Scottish side. Bob Geldof resurrected the Band-Aid single with a whole new cast of young singers to help the Ebola-stricken countries.

George Bush brought out a book about his dad and wrote on his friendship with Clinton! Ireland decided it needed an Irish fiction laureate and drew up a list of the usual suspects that nobody read.

I was walking the pup along the prom when I met a slow-moving elderly man. He raised his cane, boomed,

"Well, I declare, Jack-een Taylor."

There was no warmth in that, none at all. I didn't recognize him but nothing new in that. He was one of those who didn't see the pup. That was all I needed to know. I gave a terse,

"Hello"

Kept going.

But he wasn't done, said,

"Getting very high and mighty, are we?"

I sighed, wondered if I should just get honest, slap him in the mouth, be done with it. I looked at him, said,

"Hey, I don't know you and I have no desire to remedy that."

He smiled, showing some seriously bad teeth, said,

"I had a pub in Forster Street and you were more than a regular."

I moved to go. The pup was showing signs of maybe gnawing on the guy's leg and I wasn't sure I'd stop him. Before I could answer, he added with a smirk,

"I barred you."

That didn't really jog my memory a whole lot. I'd been barred from the best and the worst. I said,

"You take care now."

I leaned on the *care* letting it be something else entirely. He seemed reluctant to let it slide, said,

"They caught that lunatic, the guy who was killing people for speaking badly."

140

I thought, Emily will be pissed. He was on her to-do list. I looked out at the bay, dark clouds were forming on the horizon, I said,

"You need to get home before the storm."

He laughed, near spat,

"Weather never worried me."

I gave the pup a rub on his ear, turned to go, and asked,

"Who's talking about the weather?"

". . . self-dramatizing types with small, unpeopled lives."
(India Knight, writing about women who have no children)

Emily was curled up on my couch when I got back. The pup, with no fanfare, leaped onto her lap, settled down for a kip. I said,

"Feel free to break into my apartment as the feeling grabs you."

Then I saw the tears on her cheeks. I asked,

"Hey, you okay?"

She made a supreme effort, focused, then spat,

"Do I seem *okay*? But I'll be fine. I'm always fucking fine."

I let out a slow breath, said,

"Whoa, just trying to show some concern."

She rubbed the pup, said,

"Keep it for some fool who gives a fuck."

I didn't answer, let the harshness be its own resonance. She heard it, tried,

"Sorry, I'd been reading India Knight and, you know, I used to admire that cow, then she demolishes women without children with the cruelest sentence in the language."

I said,

"But you're young, you can have a whole hurling team of kids."

She scoffed, intoned,

"You see me as the mothering type. I mean, seriously?"

Hmm.

I said,

"Some breaking news: they got the Grammarian."

Got her attention. She said,

"That's awkward."

Of the many things I thought it was, that wasn't the first to spring to mind. I asked,

"Why?"

"Hard to kill the fuck in jail. Not impossible, but difficult."

To argue with her would just be wasted energy. I said,

"Let it go. If the guy is guilty, he's done."

She gave me a long look, said,

"Sometimes, you might well be the weakest shite I know."

Ouch.

I went with a smile, said,

"But you keep on coming back."

Shook her head, said,

"Don't flatter yourself, Taylor, I love the pup."

I opened the door, asked,

"If there's nothing else?"

She put her hands on her hips, glared, said,

"You don't get it, do you?"

I headed for the fridge, pulled out a longneck, and, like a good ole boy, flipped off the cap. Looked impressive, I think. Said,

"I get that you are some weird hybrid of *The Girl with the Dragon Tattoo* and Carol O'Connell's Mallory. You should read Boston Teran's *God Is a Bullet*, but alas, the novelty has worn off and I am seriously tired of you so here's the thing: fuck off."

I drank off half the bottle then moved to physically grab her and sling her. She recoiled in total ferocity, hissed,

"You put a hand on me, I will tear it from the socket and feed it to the pup."

Spittle leaked from the corners of her mouth and her eyes were locked on derangement.

She took a deep breath, said,

"This fucker, this *Grammarian*, he was part of my father's circle. You remember dear old Dad, right? Who liked to rape girls."

Phew.

I said,

"Your father is dead and any talk of a circle of . . . others . . . was never proved."

She was violently shaking her head, said,

"You seriously believe my father operated for so long on just . . . *luck*?"

I tried to keep a conciliatory tone, said,

"I understand you'd want to believe a conspiracy and keep the flame of vengeance hopping but there is one thing you have to concede."

Her eyes said she wanted to rip my head off but she went with,

"What's that?"

"He's in jail, done deal."

Now she laughed and, with fierce bitterness, asked,
"In this country you know who the best lawyers are?"
I said,
"The ones not in jail."
She ignored that, said,
"Protestants. They may have lost the land but they still have the juice and guess what, that bollix in jail is . . . da da, Protestant."
I was never going to get anywhere. I said,
"How about you get some rest?"
That lame line they trot out in B movies when they run out of script. She grabbed her bag, said,
"I'll see myself out and, oh, thanks for fucking nothing."
I fed the pup, left a bowl of water, and then took off after her. It was time to discover where she lived or stayed. She rented cars as she needed them but was now on foot.
Determined.
For a person as paranoid as she was, she didn't seem to think someone might follow her and took no precautions. I trailed her to an apartment block in Nun's Island. It was that new popular fad: gated. We had come full circle, from a country that prided itself on not locking its doors to electronic gates and security guards.
Did we feel safer?
Did we fuck?
I watched her disappear inside a three-story building and wondered who she was when she got to her own

space. Did she relinquish all the personas, let out her breath, and just be?

I'd wait until she took off somewhere and then break in. I needed to be sure she wasn't likely to return and find me as she was quite likely to shoot me. Whatever her various contradictory feelings for me, invading her space was not going to fly; she'd go berserk.

I headed back into town and all the speculation had worked up a thirst. A light fog was hovering over the city and made it seem like a serene place. Or maybe it was just so much mist. I went to Garavan's and grabbed a stool at the bar. I didn't recognize the barman and was grateful, chat was not on my agenda. Ordered a pint and a Jay. The guy knew his craft, let that pint slow-build. I held up the glass with the Jameson, the gold sheen promising so much. Never ceased to light up my hope. That what?

I'd find some peace, respite?

Not so much no more.

Those days were buried.

I was thus musing when a man stood beside me, ordered a large brandy, and let out a sigh, said to no one in particular,

"Tis a whore of a day."

He looked like, as Daniel Woodrell once wrote, sixty stiches short of handsome. He knocked back the brandy, shuddered, muttered,

"Christ."

I knew that feeling. Would it take or resurface? That pure moment of heaven and hell, then it righted and he belched, said,

"Fuck, I needed that."

Now he could settle into drinking. He got a pint and drank a healthy half, then, at last, surveyed his surroundings, me. He said,

"Grand oul day for it."

Indeed.

There would probably be an hour of bonhomie, then he'd begin spoiling for aggro. I debated on the wisdom of chancing another round before the curtain fell. He was falling into the *I love every-frigging-body,* and launched,

"I thought if I got married, nobody would notice how odd I was."

This had the feel and texture of an oft-repeated refrain, so what the hell, I could do ten minutes, I said,

"Yeah."

Neither a question nor agreement, just throw it out there. Safe. He said,

"Didn't work."

Like seriously, I could give a fuck?

I asked, sounding as if I cared,

"She left you?"

He gave me a look, bordering on pity, said,

"Don't be daft. She went round telling everybody how odd I was."

The Jay had worked some abandon and I said,

"Backfired, eh?"

Not good.

He snarled,

"What's that mean?"

Fuck.

I said,

"Tell you what: you carry on drinking and talking shite and me, I'll take my good self elsewhere."

Before he could quite digest the insult I was moving, and the barman said,

"Nice one, Jack."

Depends on which side of a good beating you sit.

I stopped to listen to a guy massacre "The Fields of Athenry," got my phone out, and called Emily.

Answering machine that went,

"Hey asshole, you know the drill."

Okay.

I said,

"Emily, got a lead on your plan for the Grammarian but it's vital you meet me at the Twelve Pins in Connemara before five this afternoon."

I got a large takeaway coffee from a deli and a half bottle of Jay, moved down to Nun's Island, and settled down in a doorway to wait.

"Cotton Point is plagued with rabid foxes, and the novel's haunting refrain '*poison fox bit you, you were poison too.*'"
(Pete Dexter, *Train*)

Superintendent Clancy had gathered the murder squad. He was caught between the prospects of landing a huge coup and a massive fuckup. He peered at the anxious faces of the Guards and detectives assembled, began,

"We stand on the precipice of a great success."

Paused.

He did like his drama.

Then,

"Or a horrendous clusterfuck."

He picked out Ridge's face, said,

"Park, the suspect, has called for a lawyer and we know what that means."

Did he expect an answer?

A guy at the back ventured,

"We have to beat the shite out of him now."

Clancy nearly smiled then reined in, barked,

"That is not how we do things."

Murmurs.

"Tear his house apart, bring me something that says this is the fellah."

Ridge tried,

"We already have lots of suspicious items but nothing that is definite. He did have an inordinate amount of dictionaries."

A moment as the crowd wondered if this was a joke. Nope.

She continued,

"The suspect seems to be disoriented. We think he administered a DIY version of ECT."

Clancy took a moment to figure this, then,

"You mean he shocked the be-Jaysus out of his own self?"

He was interrupted by a young Guard who said,

"He's lawyered up."

Said it just like in the movies. Clancy said,

"Fuck."

He snapped at the young guy,

"Is he a Prod?"

The guy did know he meant Protestant but wasn't altogether sure what one looked like. He'd grown up in the years such nonsense didn't rate, he tried,

"Should I ask him, sir?"

Clancy raised his eyes to heaven, muttered,

"Give me fucking patience."

Then to Ridge,

"Get me evidence. We'll stall this shithead as long as we can."

The lawyer, named Person, knew he had a headline case and had alerted the press, and put on his Mason's tie for the doorstep lecture he'd deliver. If he handled it the right way, he'd get a book out of this and use that to claim an artist's tax exemption. It was win-win. Clancy came out of his office, all fuss and blunder, said,

"Be just a moment while your client is having a wee cup of tea."

Pearson smiled, said,

"Well, Superintendent, it's like this: you can opt for the small fiasco or go large when I add police brutality to the sheet."

Clancy looked as though he might wallop him, then asked,

"I know you?"

Pearson gave a well-fed, well-rehearsed chuckle, then,

"Not yet but by Christ you will."

Clancy thought,

"Yeah, a Prod."

"Pain is both a tool and a working condition, like heat or a dictionary. And more important, that pain is like darkness, held at bay by the candles of our friendship and our world."

I watched Emily drive out of the gated building. She was driving an Aston Martin. She seemed to have unlimited access to cars, like everything else.

I got across the road before the gate clanged shut, and getting into the main block took a good five minutes. I had a fine-tuned set of burglar keys given to me by a guy who now sat on the new water board. Still picking people's pockets but with sanction, if not approval. The door to her apartment gave me a moment of pause. Would she booby-trap?

Oh, yeah.

So I was extremely careful, my heart hammering.

Finally the door opened and I stepped inside. An OCD wet dream. Spotless and everything in white: walls, sofas, coffee table. A lingering aroma of weed and patchouli. Not unpleasant.

There was an open-plan sitting room leading to a kitchen and bedroom. On the main wall was a large framed photo of a man with his collar turned up, heading into a dark alley. It was black-and-white and, dare I say, arresting.

"Fuck,"

I said,

As

I realized it was me.

Jesus.

Shaking my head, I headed for the kitchen, a solid steel fridge, opened to reveal a full-stocked range of supplies. Six-pack of Shiner Bock; had me one of those cold babes. Still hadn't decided if I wanted her to know she'd been invaded. On the kitchen table was this:

A solid gold Colt .45, fully loaded, ready to rock. It was a beautiful piece. Yeah, I'd confiscate it. Slid it into the waistband of my jeans. Felt better already. If she came home suddenly, I could simply shoot her.

A small shelf had some books, titles were

All My Puny Sorrows.

Probably among the finest novels ever on suicide and indeed family fuckup.

Then,

David Foster Wallace essays.

And

Anne Sexton poems.

Why was that not a surprise?

I finished the beer, thought,

"Go another?"

Yeah, why not?

Pulling drawers open at random, I found a faded photo, four men, one I recognized as Emily's murderous father and, beside him, a man whose head was circled in red, and a red label above proclaiming/ asking?

"The Grammarian?"

162

The other two I knew from a high-profile case where they had been convicted of assaulting young girls. I said,

"Fucking motley crew."

In her closet I found a metal chest, opened to see stacks of banded cash, muttered,

"Holy shit."

Tempted to grab a wedge but, hey, taking the gun, that was simply disarming her. But taking money — that was outright stealing. Put a pack in my jacket, hundreds of euros. Moved across the room and opened a closet and, oh, fuck

Reams and reams of baby clothes. I shut that quick, my heart scalded. Said,

"I am not going to think about that, no fucking way, I didn't see it."

I moved to the door, looked back at her life, barren, cold, empty, and like, I had something better?

That evening I was sitting in Garavan's, pint and chaser in play, feeling tired. I'd taken the pup for a long hike and he was now home, knackered. I was in the snug in the hope of no one bothering me. I had about as much chat in me as the government had credibility.

"Damage hardens us all. It will harden you, too, when it finds you. And it will find you."
(William Landay, *Defending Jacob*)

A woman came in, stood before me, in that indeterminate age group of forty-fifty. Well groomed, long black coiffed hair, and a face that was striking more than pretty. Her clothes quietly whispered,

"Money and, yeah, class."

I don't know if God donates class but I was pretty sure that the devil handed out style. Whatever she was selling, I didn't want it. I raised my glass, conveying,

"Take it elsewhere, lady."

She sat. I mean, fuck it, just sat. Said,

"You are Jack Taylor."

How many times I'd begun a case with just those words and never, fuck never, did it end well. I looked her right in the face, measured,

"I don't care whether your husband/dog is missing or whatever, your son/daughter/ . . . you hear me? I can't help you."

She was unfazed, just leveled those lovely sad eyes on me, said,

"It's my nephew, Parker Wilson."

Name rang a bell but I couldn't be bothered figuring it, said,

"Please go away. Find somebody who gives a rat's arse."

She leaned into me, said,

"They are calling him the Grammarian."

Whoa.

Had to do a whole double take, then,

"Well, lady, he is fucked, signed, sealed, and delivered. Get him a good lawyer, cop for insanity."

She sat back, took me in with a full eye search, and nothing warm was there. She said,

"You have a rep for finding information that the Guards can't."

I shrugged, said,

"You need a miracle, I don't do miraculous."

She put a fat envelope on the counter, said,

"I believe you can be . . . bought."

Was I outraged?

Indignant.

Nope.

I could be bought — and cheaply.

I asked,

"What is it you want?"

As I asked, the strangest feeling hit me. I began to feel a tingle all along my spine, as if someone trod heavily on my grave, and fuck, barely recognized the feeling, it had been so long, so dormant.

Attraction.

Ah, shite, I needed that like a wallop to the head. My mind muttering,

"No way, no fucking way, not going through all the shit again."

Even as my treacherous heart began to sing. And I swear, she saw it, in that uncanny way that women have. A tiny smile at the corner of the mouth as she sussed it.

She said,

"My name is Sarah, Sarah Compton, and I want you to prove that Park is innocent."

Piece of cake.

All biz, I asked,

"Where is he now?"

She looked at her watch, slim Rolex, said,

"Just about making bail."

As Park was being released, Sergeant Ridge was standing beside him, whispered,

"Enjoy the brief outing. I'll have your arse back in here so quick . . ."

He looked at her like a total stranger, then murmured,

"Mind your language."

Sarah had a car arranged and before the press could engulf him she had him in the back and sped away with cameras flashing at its taillights. Park's mind was beginning to settle but words and letters still created a small rainbow at the edge of his vision. He said to Sarah, vague distress lining his tone,

"All the letters are lowercase."

She looked to see if the driver had heard, then said,

"We're going to bring you to my house. It's peaceful there."

He was quiet for a bit, then asked,

"Do you have a Fowler's *Modern English Usage* there?"
She thought,
"Uh-oh."
Said,
"Park, best if you concentrate on getting rest for now."
He closed his eyes for a moment, then said,
"Lowercase implies capital catastrophe is imminent."
Sarah thought,
"Mad as a hatter."
But family.

"It was a gesture of forgiveness that had everything to do with the forgiver and little to do with the forgiven. It was forgiveness as powerful arrogance."
(Gideon Lewis-Kraus, *A Sense of Direction*)

"The art of punctuation is of infinite consequence in writing; as it contributes to the perspicuity and consequently to the beauty of every composition."

This edict of Joseph Robertson was running through Park's mind like good news. He knew it signaled a return to his former self and his dormant energy. His aunt Sarah had fussed over settling him in the guest room, insisting,

"Rest, you need to rest."

"No."

He thought,

"I need to kill somebody."

And he remembered how the female sergeant had scoffed at his language, had sneered,

"Afraid of a little bad grammar, are we?"

The construction of that sentence infuriated him and the casual way she abused and tore apart the very basics of structure revealed the barbarian she was.

He lay on the bed and ran the rudiments of his favorite linguistics, and running alongside this pleasure was the idea of shutting the Guard's mouth permanently. He asked aloud,

. . . "Affect or effect?"

I.e.,

The sergeant was affected by the effect of the hatchet.

Emily was standing in the center of my apartment, so enraged that the pup hid under a chair. Loud voices freaked him; didn't do a whole lot for me either.

Like this,

"My place was burgled, you believe it?"

Oh, I not only believed; I *knew*. When she was in full riot, her eyes seemed bright green. She was spitting from anger, continued,

"Going through my private stuff, and you know who did it?"

A question or a touch of rhetoric?

I frowned accordingly. She threw her hands in the air. Spat,

"That cunt cop."

Whoa . . .

I asked,

"What?"

"Ridge, the gay bitch, she's had it in for me since I rubbed her nose in it."

Had to close this down, said,

"Seriously, I don't think breaking and entering is part of their remit."

She spun around, eyes spitting iron.

"Ah, you dumb, deluded sap."

Couldn't let that go, said,

"I don't think they use *sap* outside of earnest chick lit."

Then she had a sea change, touched my face, tenderly, her eyes now soft, said,

"Ah, Jack."

And a lightbulb went on. I realized something.

She

     Had

         Feelings

             For me.

Oh, sweet fuck.

How could I not have seen? The huge framed photo on her wall. Always there for me. As I tried to process this, she asked quietly,

"Jack, can we talk?"

Lord above.

I resolved, in my utter blindness, to let her down easy.

Aw, fuck, the arrogance and sheer stupidity. If only I could blame drink, dope, stress, but no, it was all on me, my total lack of *cop on* is absolutely appalling. I have no excuse save pure bollix.

Me.

I said (oh, the generosity and sensitivity!),

"Let's go and have dinner, my treat, and we can talk."

I cringe as I recall the smugness of my tone.

She said,

"Oh, thank you, jack. I knew you'd get it."

My name in lowercase there as that is how small I feel now.

"4-play they called themselves, as what they had in common was child molestation and golf. Oh, and an utter contempt for the human race."

I need to see Emily's mother and find out about the four in the picture. Two had been convicted of sexual offenses and, as is the case now with Irish justice, they were on holiday in Marbella, awaiting appeals. Emily's father was dead and that left Park Wilson, the alleged Grammarian. I needed transport and knocked on my neighbor Doc's door. He had been many times in my apartment but I had never set foot in his. He had a fairly new Austin and that would do my trip nicely.

The pup was on his lead and his tail wagging gently as I knocked. Took a few minutes and then the door opened a fraction, the way you do for TV license inspectors, giving not an inch. Doc's head appeared. Looking startled, he gasped,

"What?"

Fuck, not a good sign, he had never been anything but warmly friendly. The pup tried to push in but Doc snapped,

"Not now."

Sharp.

Jesus.

Maybe I could rent a bloody car.

I said,

"Really sorry to disturb you."

He actually went,

"Whatever!"

Now if ever a comment deserved a slap in the mouth, it's that. I tried,

"I was hoping to borrow your car, I'll pay for the petrol and . . ."

He cut me off, muttered,

"Jesus."

Went back inside and did I hear a whispered conversation?

Then he was back, handed me the keys, and shut the door. The pup stared at the door, crushed, his tail beneath his legs. I said,

"Ah, fuck him, come on, we'll have a wild spin."

Thing with dogs, they instantly forgive but they don't forget.

Me neither.

The Grammarian would kill me for that sentence.

I put the pup in the shotgun seat and then went,

"Ah, for fuck's sake."

Not the pup, not a stick shift. Damn automatic. I could with some difficulty manage but said to the pup,

"Gonna be a bumpy ride."

He seemed to trust me. I said to him,

"See, the old ways, they had some style. Did I ever tell you of the old Galway cures?"

He turned his head to the side so I figured, no. I began,

Baldness: Beef bone marrow rubbed on the bald pate.

Corns: Paraffin oil on cotton wool and rub in slowly like sarcasm.

I swear the pup found that amusing.

Chesty cough: Hot water in a mug with honey and a mass of carrageen moss.

Toothache: Drop of Jameson with salt added and rub gently on the gums. If that failed, drink more Jay.

The radio was playing and a news bulletin, P. D. James had died.

RIP.

She wasn't exactly noted for her sense of humor but, at a book signing, in Australia, a long line of people and with each customer she tried to write the buyer's name and have a word.

One woman handed over the book and when P. D. asked, she wasn't sure she could spell the name correctly but gave it her best shot

. . . Emma Chessit.

As she handed back the book, she realized the woman was asking the price of the book.

I'd once given a copy of

An Unsuitable Job for a Woman

To Ridge.

In the days when we were still friends, before the death of our beloved friend, Stewart, Ridge had asked me to suggest some crime novels and she had loved James Lee Burke

Hilary Davidson

Patti Abbott

Sara Gran

So, emboldend, I'd given her the P. D. James and she stared at the title, snarled,

"What? You trying to tell me something, Taylor?"

Ah, just fuck off already.

A Swollen Red Sun

By Matthew McBride, which is among my ten favorites, I decided she would not now be getting. Let her go back to fucking chick lit.

Emily's mother's house was still bright, clean, and alive. So, still sober, then.

I left the radio on for the pup, a few treats, said,

"Back in a sec, buddy."

He looked as if that seemed unlikely. I approached the door with a certain amount of trepidation. Rang the bell, and in a beat, there she was. She asked,

"Yes?"

"I am so sorry to bother you. I'm a friend of Em . . ."

Didn't get to finish. She rasped,

"Taylor."

Uh-oh.

Not good.

I tried,

"So sorry to disturb you."

"No, you're not, otherwise you wouldn't be here."

Fuck . . . Okay . . . deep breath.

Think I liked her better as a drunk.

She stared past me, asked,

"What kind of person leaves a pup locked in a car?"

Jesus.

She motioned for me to get him, and added,

"Wipe your feet."

To, I suppose, accessorize her wiping the floor with me. I could have of course just said,

"Aw, fuck off."

And fucked off me own self.

But I never
> Never
>> Know
>>> When
>>>> To
>>>>> Quit.

Her house was spotless, OCD in huge evidence or maybe just being sober. She got a biscuit and broke it in half for the pup. She asked,

"What is his name?"

In a futile attempt at humor, to lighten the mood, I used the line from my favorite western:

"Never name something you might have to eat."

Whoops.

She glared at me, spat,

"That's not even remotely amusing."

Phew-oh.

I noticed a framed print with the words

KISS

The acronym KISS is applied from principles of business, advertising, computer systems. Einstein said, "Everything should be made as simple as possible but not too simple."

Like most alkies I had a passing knowledge of AA slogans but this was new to me. She saw me looking at it, asked,

"You know who wrote that?"

"Einstein?"

She literally puckered her lips in dismissal, said,

"My dear friend Parker Wilson, the poor man they are accusing of horrendous things."

Which is the whole reason for my visit and now I had an in. I asked,

"You knew him well?"

"Define well."

Fuck me, I definitely liked her better as a meek drunk. This new abrasive bitch was beginning to piss me off. I went offensive.

"Not a difficult question and, might I say, you seem to have come on in leaps and bloody bounds."

She sighed as in,

"God spare me imbeciles."

Said,

"My therapist stressed I need to be assertive."

I nearly laughed, said,

"Trust me, it's working."

She rubbed the pup's ears. That eased me a bit, not a lot, but climbing down, she said,

"My late husband, Park, and two other men had a group based on golf, sex, and money, and they rather fetchingly called themselves 4-Play."

Fetchingly!

I snarled,

"Was this before or after your husband molested your daughter?"

Bull's-eye.

Her face crumbled, the force behind her eyes dimming, and she looked as though she might fall down.

I could give a good fuck.

She tried,

"I didn't know, I couldn't have known, I thought she was just . . ."

Um.

". . . a quiet child."

I let that hover before I shot,

"The wife never knows, eh? And now you *do* know and you have a saying by one of his . . ."

I had to search for the word:

"*Mates*

Displayed on your fucking wall."

She said, very quietly,

"Please don't curse."

I took a deep breath, then,

"I know two of the men, in a photo Emily has, were already arrested, your husband is . . . um . . . out of the picture, so that leaves Wilson, and I have been asked to try and clear his name."

She stared at me in amazement, uttered,

"You?"

I said, with tight control,

"It's what I do."

She pondered this, then,

"They all drank a great deal and I've learned in my program that normal inclinations become perverted by alcohol."

Fuck's sake.

I said,

"Blame the demon drink, eh?"

A thin, mean smile danced along her lower lip. She said,

"One feels you have experienced some demons of your own."

Bitch.

I gave up, said,

"Here's my mobile number. If you think of anything that might help your *friend's* defense, I would be grateful."

I called the pup, who decided to show off and made an impressive leap into my arms.

Who knew?

I was at the door when she said,

"I would like to say it's been a pleasure but I have learned that honesty is essential. It says so in *The Big Book of Alcoholics Anonymous.*"

I looked at her, the smug expression, figuring she'd scored the last point, and said,

"That same book talks about a state of mind that I think you may have."

"Oh, and what might that be, Mr. Taylor?"

I let the moment build, then,

"A state of mind that only can be described as savage."

" 'The king died and then the queen died,' is a story.
'The king died, and then the queen died of grief' is a plot."
(E. M. Forster, *Aspects of the Novel*)

Park's aunt Sarah had a conference with the lawyer representing him.

You get what you pay for and, in this case, as she was laying out a shitload of green, she had the whiz kid of the city. But smarmy.

Oh, yeah.

Sarah knew to be suspicious of any man who wore more jewelry than she did. And not only that, but classy gear. And he did that annoying thing of shooting his cuffs to emphasize a point and, of course, to show you the Cartier watch, etc.

His office alone cost as much as the salaries of the Irish Water Board. And he was just as arrogant as those charlatans. He said,

"I've been in touch with Sergeant Ridge. She is the chief cop on the case and a dyke."

Sarah wanted to ask,

"And this sexual data helps . . . how?"

But every question cost another five hundred euros. She nodded sagely. Not easy when you did not wish to draw attention to your double chin. He continued,

"It seems our boy used to give himself ECT."

She thought,

"What?"

The lawyer smiled and this had the effect of her checking to see if she maybe had something stuck in her teeth. He said,

"If we go the insanity route, this will be a huge advantage."

Then he suddenly stood up, majestic in the movement, spluttered,

"Good gracious, where are my manners?"

He had the Trinity accent that those who attended in the '70s acquired. Not quite posh but cultured, showed learning more than breeding. It let you know they were indeed better but not showy with it.

"Coffee, tea, we have Earl Grey and Darjeeling."

She refused, wanted to get to the bottom line. He continued,

"Our Mr. Wilson administered a voltage of five hundred watts to his brain on frequent occasions. You might say his mind was indeed scrambled."

Sarah was, dare I say, shocked. She made a small

"Oh."

The lawyer seemed to think this was appropriate and said,

"Mind you, there is now a bracelet on the market that gives you three hundred forty watts. It comes as a black rubber wristband with an LED light buried inside it; they are calling it a wearable personal trainer. Two copper terminals deliver the current with a simple two-second warning."

Sarah was aghast, wondering if he was *trying to sell one to her*. She asked,

"Good heavens, why?"

He chuckled, genuinely amused, said,

"It's named the Pavlov bracelet after the Russian who conditioned the dogs."

This she knew about but she was mystified, said,

"I am mystified."

He elaborated,

"It is designed to stop us yielding to our addictions."

Sarah was shaking her head. He tried to elucidate.

"Invented by a Stanford whiz kid of the name Maneesh Sethi, it sells at a price of three hundred euros."

He waited and when she had nothing, said,

"We can use this to show that Park, though obviously off his fucking head . . ."

She jumped at the obscenity as he intended. He liked to have her full attention. Then,

"Was at least trying to, shall we say, cure himself."

She was dubious, asked,

"And that would, um, fly?"

He laughed again, a more brutal tone having leaked across his words, said,

"It's bullshit but at least it shows he is at worst a harmless eccentric."

Sarah didn't know if this meant that Park would walk or be confined so she asked,

"What are his chances?"

Lawyers love, just fucking love, questions, and the sillier the better, plus, a long answer stretches out those billable hours, as he'd learned from *Boston Legal*. He saw himself with the cachet of William Shatner and the chutzpah of James Spader. He'd learned those two c words in the past week and used them frequently. He adopted that lawyerly look, eyes above the pince-nez so you thought you were seeing double. You were certainly *paying* double, and said,

"If we draw Judge Fahy, we are in with a shout because she is *très* simpatico to madness. The worst would be Bennett. He let two rapists walk recently and is determined to jail some poor bastard."

Sarah was still lost, said,

"The press are camped outside my home."

He shrugged that away — not his problem — said,

"Thing is to try and make our dear Park appear . . ."

He cleared his throat, noisily, then,

". . . Normal."

She gave a cynical shrug, as in,

"Good frigging luck with that."

He nearly smiled but went with,

"Couldn't you get him a copy of Lynne Truss and let him, I don't know, be seen with that and somehow have the focus on his intellectual side?"

She had no idea of who that person was but this was why God invented Google.

She stood up, said,

"Thank you."

He stood, too, had to now that he might be a hoot but at least a hoot with manners. For a horrible moment she thought he might actually kiss her hand. He said,

"*C'est ne pas rien.*"

" 'Call me Ishmael.' She stared blankly,
then grinned. 'I'm going to hit the
keg — need a refill?' He sighed. No
one reads anymore."
(Frank Byrns, "Talking of Michelangelo")

Storm Rachel finally hit, the west coast worst of all. Howling winds, snow, ice, monsoon rain, power cuts, and flooded homes, all the usual outriders of Armageddon in a green wave. The pup doesn't really do storms or, indeed, most bad weather. He hides under the sofa with my Galway GAA hurling shirt as a security blanket. I'd have gone in there with him if there was room.

But hey, I had a date. No wonder the elements were deranged. A rib broke in the devil. I tried to envision my own face when Emily told me she loved me. Christ, let me be humble and gracious, and let the bitch down easy.

I did neither

Humility

Grace

Nor

Niceness with any conviction. In fact, I usually seemed to be about to vomit. But she might cancel owing to the storm.

She didn't.

Left a message on my phone

"Hey, babe, the G Grill at eight, dress to fascinate."

Right.

As the winds battered against the window, the pup glared at me, like,

"Why have you not stopped the storm?"

I said,

"I'm working on it, buddy."

I put on a new crisp white shirt. Fuck, why do they put all those frigging pins in there and you always miss one which lacerates the tender part of your neck. I loose managed a Rotary club tie, me being one of the very few who they actually voted not to allow to join. A black waistcoat to give me the crime writer's vibe, my washed 501s.

Then the pièce de résistance.

Doc Martens,

Which I had done the impossible with: got a shine on there.

Hid the steel toe caps.

And finally, my all-weather Garda coat. It had been

Burned

Thrashed

Beaten

Usually with me in it.

The G Grill was the latest flash place in town and not even a storm of such ferocity could dent its allure. I reluctantly had to leave the pup alone as my neighbor Doc wasn't answering. Most of the floodwater still clogged the main street but the ubiquitous buskers were undaunted, one so enterprising as to have a sign,

"Feel guilty about Katrina? Now is your chance to catch up."

I gave him a ten for ingenuity and I swear he shouted,

"Yo, bro, get the boxed set of *Treme*."

I looked at him, dressed like the joker in *The Dark Knight*, down to the horror makeup. I asked,

"You watch box sets?"

Like he had a home?

He smiled with that grim Heath Ledger smile, said,

"Get real, bro, streaming, it be the way."

That he rasped like Bob Marley only added to the surreal tone. I carried on. Met Des Kenny, trailing off the end of his marathon.

Fuck.

Here was the oligarch of Irish bookselling, dressed in shorts and Lifeboats T-shirt, looking fit and healthy. I asked,

"You're running now?"

He gave that radiant grin, said,

"Aw, Jack, we can't all simply stand still."

Deep.

He asked,

"Got a hot date, boyo?"

Heat all right.

The G Grill had a guy on the door, a guy with bags of attitude. He stepped in front of me, asked,

"Help you?"

Fuck's sake.

I said,

"Doubt it."

He flexed his gym pecs, smiled, thinking,

"Player."

But another guy stepped forward, said,

"Jack, how's it cutting?

I knew him from a brief stint I did as a security guard. We'd had some drinks and shot the shit. He looked like Jeremy Kyle, which was a hell of handicap. Kyle is the TV guy, a poor man's Jerry Springer, makes his living shouting at folks from disadvantaged backgrounds.

I said,

"Going okay until this asshole got in my face."

Jeremy smiled as the guy bristled, said,

"They're keen is all."

The guy tried,

"Boss, we can't have riffraff hanging around."

I breezed past the guy, his hands itching to clout me. Jeremy said,

"Have a cocktail on the house."

I nearly smiled, said,

"Far from cocktails I was reared."

He shrugged, his eyes scanning the room, like what he saw on *NCIS*. I asked,

"This your living now?"

Couldn't stop the vague contempt that leaked over my tone.

He did that body look, head to toe, that sneers,

"You actually bought that shit you're wearing? How cheap are you?"

Before I could answer, he added,

"Thing is, Jack-o, there's great opportunity in the security biz and you, being once a Guard and all, you could nail down some serious change."

All this crap in a quasi-American accent. I shook my head, moved to the bar, got a double Jay in, then saw what appeared to be a young Deborah Harry waving at me from the dining room.

Emily.

Jesus.

Jeremy looked at her, asked in disbelief,

"You snaring that, huh?"

"Go away,"

I said.

I knocked back the Jay, headed for Blondie. She rose to greet me, did the frigging air kiss, exclaimed,

"Jack, you look . . ."

Searched for a word,

Got,

"Different."

I said,

"You have that Debbie Harry gig down."

Sounding not un-American my own self.

Shit is infectious.

"Who?"

Right.

She seemed up, energized, and I felt bad at how I was going to blow her buzz.

Rain on her parade.

Shit on her doorstep.

Well, you get my drift.

She said,

"Punctuation is so important."

WTF?

Was everyone obsessed with grammar? I ignored that, asked, as if I cared,

"How'd you survive the storm?"

This seemed to amuse her highly and she said first,

"You have to know that men name storms and they're always female. Why is that?"

I tried a half-arsed smile myself, said,

"The ferocity and, I suppose, the unpredictability."

We sat at a table as we waited to be summoned to our dinner. A woman appeared, dressed in black waistcoat, ultra-white blouse, short black skirt, and driller heels. She said,

"Good evening, folks, I will be your server slash host this pleasant occasion and anything you need, don't hesitate to call."

I sighed.

We had truly adopted most of the U.S. culture. I said,

"Couple drinks would be a start."

She almost glared. I was not the type of diner she anticipated. She ran with it, addressing Emily, cooed,

"Would madam wish to peruse the cocktail menu?"

Madam would not.

Snapped,

"Jack Daniel's on the rocks, twist of lemon."

In bourbon?

Was JD even bourbon or sour mash?

I had the Jay, no rocks. Emily fixed her gaze on me, said,

"I was thinking of you last night as I was reading."
Uh-huh.
I gave her my interested look, which basically reads,
"Bore me."
She continued,
"John Kennedy Toole, David Foster Wallace, both suicides and both with controlling mamas."
Did she require an answer?
She did.
I said,
"As I had the mother from hell and I don't write, why would you think of me?"
The drinks came and Emily looked at her glass, asked,
"Is that lemon fresh?"
Our server muttered something vague and fucked off. I felt her love of us was waning. Emily returned to her searching scrutiny of me, asked.
"Did you ever consider the big thing?"
Ah, fuck, where was the declaration of adoration in this? I said,
"Not a day goes by."
She was intrigued, pushed,
"And?"
"Who'd mind the pup?"
She took out her e-cig, blew vapor, and I said,
"I was watching *The Border* Season Two, and a drug lord described those things as gay cigarettes."
She laughed at that and it was good to hear that spontaneous sound. Then, surfing that, she near gushed,
"Jack, I was going to wait until after dinner but I have to tell you now."

Finally.

"Jack, I have fallen in love with someone."

I tried to look, I don't know,

Expectant?

Happy?

Humble?

She almost whispered,

"It's Doc."

"What?"

She beamed, radiant.

"Oh, I knew you'd be delighted."

I muttered,

"Delighted?"

She reached for my hand, her face a riot of joy, said,

"It's so perfect. When I move in with him, we'll be like . . ."

Reached for the horrible fucking word.

"Neighbors."

I snatched back my hand, as if bitten, said,

"Neighbors?"

She was beginning to catch on, asked,

"Aren't you happy for me?"

I tried to bite down, not go ballistic, settled for,

"Isn't he . . ."

With utter sarcasm, leaned on,

"*LIKE*,

. . . a tad fucking old for you?"

Our server arrived, happy to announce,

"Your table is ready, folks."

Almost in chorus we went,

"Fuck off."

"We have a language that is full of ambiguities; we have a way of expressing ourselves that is often complex and allusive, poetic and modulated. All our thoughts can be rendered with absolute clarity if we bother to put the right dots and squiggles between the words in the right places." (Lynne Truss)

I disappeared.

Utterly

Completely

Disastrously.

Post Emily, and I mean hours after, I got in touch with the only nun I knew.

Sister Maeve. She'd asked me for assistance in a very nasty, vicious case years before. It went like most of my work.

Apeshit, down the doomed toilet.

People got badly hurt but, somehow, Maeve got the result she was seeking and gave most of the credit to God and maybe ten percent to me. Enough to have her grateful. Few more valuable assets than a thankful nun. Ask the Vatican.

She agreed to mind the pup for a time; how long I didn't know. Maeve had the completely unlined face habitual to her calling. And such peaceful eyes as if she had seen the total plan. She said,

"I will be happy to have the company of this little fellah for a while."

Best of all, the pup liked her.

Back at the apartment, I was grabbing what hidden cash I had, decided to leave the gun. I was feeling so dark, it would be too much of a lure. I wore my Garda coat as stormy weather of a personal type was very much on the cards. I looked around the place; even my bookcase gave no comfort. I was just about to leave when a knock at the door. Opened it to Doc.

Who looked?

Apprehensive?

I spat,

"What?"

"May I come in?"

"No, I'm just leaving."

He tried to see over my shoulder, asked,

"Where's the pup?"

"The fuck do you care, asshole?"

He seemed crushed, tried,

"Is this about Em?"

"Em! When do you get to call her that?"

He tried another tack, said,

"Look, I know it's a surprise and we should have said something before this but, cross my heart, it took us as much by surprise."

I brushed past him, said,

"Have a nice life."

He shouted,

"Shouldn't you be happy for her?"

Jesus, nearly a clean getaway. I stopped, said, real quiet,

"I'd have thought you might be more comfortable with someone your own age."

He put his hand on me. I looked at his hand and he withdrew, said,

"Okay, I get it. You're protective, but in time you'll come around and, you know, I was hoping you might do me the honor of being my best man."

Aw, sweet Lord. I stared at him for one long moment then spun on my heel and left. I was halfway along Shop Street when a guy stepped in front of me, said,

"Cheer up, fellah, it's nearly Christmas."

I said,

"So much to look forward to, I'm dizzy with choice."

"To fully mutilate grammar you
need to firstly study it obsessively."
(Owen Daglish)

Odd times in my blasted life, I would meet a thin weather-beaten man who,

Rumor had it,

Was a mid-list crime author (i.e., didn't sell)

And had served time in jail in South America.

We had a slightly civil acquaintanceship and had shared the rare pint and even rarer to rarest conversation.

He was to be the last person I spoke to in Galway before my great escape.

He was wearing a pea jacket with the collar turned up, and an air of violence barely suppressed emanated from his whole being, but the strangest thing was

. . . That vibe seemed to be turned in on himself.

I said,

"How are you doing?"

The question amused him, as we stood on a deserted street after a raging storm. He said,

"I'm doing what little I can to stay on the dry side of things."

Me neither.

I asked,

"And how is that working for you?"

He leveled his gaze on me. Ferocity without malice, said,

"It manages to pose as normalcy."

I thought,

"Fuck, enough shite talk."

And moved on.

He called after me,

"Jack, you can run but the road is always a dead end."

Way too freaking deep.

I looked back and he was gone. I thought, not for the first time, that he was mostly fiction, a rumor pretending to be relevant.

I missed Stewart in so many ways. He had been, in just about every form, the one true friend I ever had. A former dope dealer who served five harsh years in prison. On release he reinvented himself as a Zen entrepreneur. No, not selling Zen but immersing himself in business with Zen as his fallback.

He had been by my side in so many horrendous cases and though we fought like tinkers, a deep and wild friendship endured. Sergeant Ridge was part of our unholy trinity and she and Stewart had become as tight as fleas.

He never gave up on me despite my constant ripping and ragging on him. Ridge believed my total lack of care and downright negligence had resulted in Stewart being cut in half with a shotgun blast.

She said,

"The very sight of you makes me want to vomit."
I tried,
"Don't hold back."
And she came as close to walloping me as is feasible.
Fleeing Galway now, I wondered if Stewart would have tried to prevent me.
My heart scalded in my chest as I felt his utter loss sweep over me.

"A split infinitive has much in common with a split head. Both hurt like hell."

Park looked around his aunt's home. Somewhere in his still clouded mind he knew he should be grateful for her help. She got him out on bail, secured a lawyer, let him stay in her house. But there were restrictions. She'd said,

"Best if you don't go out."

What kind of sentence was that?

It wasn't just flouting grammar. Worse, it was as if she didn't even care. He said aloud,

"They have to care and they will . . . care."

The policewoman,

Ridge?

She danced before his eyes like words he couldn't articulate. And he knew all words needed to be articulated, otherwise they atrophied. She'd mocked him, mocked grammar, and, with malice aforethought, deliberately mangled and mutilated the most basic rules of common speech.

She'd sneered,

"You'll get your due."

. . . Due to

. . . means caused by,

With a second meaning of
. . . "owing to,
because of."
He said,
"She will die because of her manner due to an irate
man."
And he smiled.
Thought,
"I am definitely on the mend."
The rules were their own reward, but the bonus and
beauty were that they seemed to reach out and
eradicate the errors. His mind went then on a tortured
circuit of reference and distraction, settling on the
wonderful wordsmith
Violet Asquith.
Now there was a lady who not only grasped the
alchemy of language but implemented it to describe
and dissect.
As in her famous description of Churchill:
"He rose like a trout to the fly of any phrase."
There was a pack of cigarettes on the kitchen table.
He wondered if he smoked. Gave it a shot, coughed,
and decided he didn't. He was staring at the coffee
machine, a sleek state-of-the-art contraption and, of
course, no instructions unless you read Japanese. The
front door opened and Sarah came in, bearing parcels.
She jumped when she saw him. He thought,
"Was I to be confined to my room?"
Followed by the not altogether thought,
"She is afraid of me."
Fear was good, it was cleansing. She said,

"I took the liberty of getting you some clothes."

Then, seeing him before the coffee machine, asked if he'd like some. He said he would and she busied herself at that, making inane small talk that he didn't understand, like weather and the price of everything. Placing a mug before him, she asked if he was hungry.

He stared at her, said,

"The word *preposition* means 'something that is placed before.' It is its function to show where one thing is in position to another."

She gave a weak smile.

"How little importance they place on the rules,"

He thought.

He asked,

"May I borrow the car?"

Startling her. She fumbled with the coffee things, then said,

"I'm not sure that is a good idea."

He looked at her in genuine astonishment, asked,

"Did I ask what you thought?"

Her expression now confirmed she was indeed very afraid. He stood up, said,

"Good coffee, now keys please."

Sarah watched him as he drove off in her relatively new BMW. She wasn't sure which worried her more, him or her car. Crossed her mind to call the Guards but that would be counterproductive. She'd learned that in a class she'd taken on self-assertion. The class didn't cover the . . .

"Possible serial killer staying in your home"

Scenario.

She called the lawyer instead and was put on hold for ten minutes. Finally the lawyer came on, sounding definitely testy. Went,

"This better be important."

She sighed. The rate she was paying this prick, he could at least be civil. She decided to try some of the assertive shtick, snapped,

"I'm not one of those frivolous people who run to the law at every minor event."

Sounded kind of, like, lame?

Now he sighed, said,

"Whatever."

She told him about Park and the car.

He asked,

"How did he seem?"

Seem?

She near screamed,

"Seem? He seemed crazy is what he seemed."

The soothing tones that cost the big bucks came into play as he purred,

"Now, now, we don't want to be throwing around those kinds of words, do we?"

A question?

She took a deep breath, didn't help, said,

"He was rambling on about punctuation."

She thought she heard a chuckle.

"He wanted nothing, for the time being,
except to understand . . .
Without advice, assistance or plan, he began
reading an incongruous assortment of books;
he would find some passage which he could
not understand in one book, and he would
get another on that subject . . .
There was no order in his reading; but there
was order in what remained of his mind."
(Ayn Rand, *The Fountainhead*)

It's not easy to simply lose a month. But I had experience. One way or another, I'd been losing bits of myself all my life. In increments, as they say. I began my binge in Garavan's on Shop Street in Galway and ended up in a dive on Kilburn High Road. Took the scenic route.

I was as usual on the opposite side of the current thinking. I was the guy who went to the graveyard on a sunny day while the world headed for the beach. Everybody and his nephew were searching for *themselves*. My mission, and *I had chosen to accept it, was to lose all*.

I can vaguely recall taking a room in Whelan's Hotel in Dublin and cutting that short when I realized it had live music *nightly*. That is every single night. Music is a bad distraction when you are studiously avoiding guilt. I was drowning in clichés. *If you are going to do just one thing, do it the best you can.*

Right.

Dublin confused me. It was, on the surface, friendly, but only apparently. You were always a *culchie*. Not of the city. I didn't help my case by sneering at their hurling team on a fairly regular basis. Was I looking for a fight? At every turn.

One memorable evening, and I use the description loosely, I sat in Neary's on Chatham Street. Like all Dublin pubs, south of the river, it tended to boast some literary connection. I think it was Patrick Kavanagh that occasion and I had mocked,

"Apart from 'On Raglan Road,' what else is he remembered for?"

The lady in my company that evening knew nowt of Kavanagh or, indeed, "On Raglan Road." I was at my most vicious, said,

"No doubt you are in mourning since *Desperate Housewives* finished."

She'd given me a long look, said,

"You have a limp, a hearing aid, mutilated fingers, and you are insulting me?"

I think I laughed, went,

"Sorry, Sheila."

"It's Maura."

Indeed.

That was Dublin.

London was cold and bitter, in every sense. Most of it I recall as dark pubs and darker people. Desperation is its own beacon and I seemed to attract the worst and the worthless. Insane conversations with the walking insane. A night in Notting Hill, in what used to be, I think, Finches, telling some arsehole,

Like this,

"I used to be a Guard."

Him.

"Like, in security?"

He could give a fuck but I was buying rounds so he could fake an interest. I said,

"No, the police."

He was in his late fifties and, like me, on the run from himself. He was, he said, or used to be,

"Something in the City."

This is the same gig as being an Internet consultant. I tuned him out for a bit as I watched the horror of *Charlie Hebdo* play out in Paris. It seemed as unreal and awful as my life.

ISIS beheaded another hostage and I told myself I was well out of a world that was so crazy and merciless. Bizarre note: If I saw someone walking a dog, I felt convulsed with guilt. And in the UK, it's nigh impossible not to see that happen many times a day. Maybe it was some weird loneliness but I took to walking along Kilburn High Road in a vague desire to hear Irish accents. Futile, as a myriad of international voices drowned out even the traffic.

And then.

They say if you walk in London long enough, you will meet just about everybody you ever knew. Fanciful and statistically impossible but a nice notion. My money was taking a hammering and thus preoccupied, I didn't at first recognize my own name.

"Jack. Jack Taylor!"

Drinking like I'd been, you begin to ignore voices as you suspect they are mostly internal and never the messengers of anything good. Kept going until my arm was grabbed. I thought,

"Nicked and about time."

Turned to see Father Malachy, the bane of my past life. We had some history and all of it bad. He'd been one of those priests who attach themselves to old women and seep in piety together to the detriment of all. I'd once memorably helped him out and was he grateful?

Was he fuck?

I almost didn't recognize him as he was in civilian clothes, quite a smart suit and heavy overcoat. He still had that priest air; it trails behind them like bad news. Not sanctity as much as superciliousness. I asked,

"Did they defrock you finally?"

He threw away a cigarette he'd been drawing on. He was one of those incorrigible smokers, smoked during a smoke. In a weird way, I was kind of glad to see him and that shows the depth of my desperation. He said,

"Who are you on the run from, Taylor?"

I nearly laughed. He was unchanged and, in a world of darkness, he had at least stayed true to his nature. I indicated a pub on the corner, asked,

"You want to grab a pint?"

He gave me that ecclesiastical stare, long on disapproval and short on compassion, and said,

"I'll consider it penance."

The bar was quiet, one middle-aged guy tending who greeted,

"Fathers."

Irish.

They can spot the clergy at close range. That he thought I was one was just more insult to my burdened mind. We ordered some pints and chasers. The guy said,

"Grab a table and I'll shoot them over to ye."

We sat and Malachy reached for his cigs. I cautioned,

"You can't smoke here."

He tried defiance for a moment then decided not to. When the drinks came, he sank the Jay fast, belched, said,

"Ah."

I know the feeling, nothing else quite like it, a split second when the world lights up and you have such peace, then . . .

He asked,

"Why are you hiding out in this heathen land?"

He still spoke like a character from Synge. I said,

"Bit of a break."

He snickered, started on his pint, said,

"I'm here for a symposium on church and communication."

He thought for a moment, added,

"Whatever the fuck a symposium is."

His face took on that flush of the habitual drinker. It could almost pass for ruddy health, seen from a certain angle. He said,

"I don't think I hate you anymore, Taylor."

I said,

"Makes me feel all warm."

He was ready for another round, shouted,

"Bring more drink."

Then,

"I used to think you were an arrogant drunkard who was the death of his sainted mother."

There was a time when I might have argued the toss but now I simply didn't care, said,

"To tell the truth, *Father*, your feelings of me never mattered a good shite to me."

We continued in this vein for another round, softly exchanging insults. Then he got a wistful look, sighed, asked,

"Did you ever experience love?"

First, I put it down to drink talk and was about to be scathing when I realized he was deadly serious. I stalled by draining my pint, then,

"Years ago, there was a child, she had Down syndrome . . ."

I trailed off, couldn't revisit the death of Serena-May, who had died on my watch or, rather, my absolute lack of watch. He actually listened, which was rare. Priests take confessions, have parishioners come with their troubles, but listen?

Not since the penal days.

He said,

"I have never known it."

I was going to try, *Surely the love of God*, but his expression was so serious that I went with,

"My mother."

Nearly choked on this but persisted,

"My mother, um, seemed, to *like* you well enough."

He gave a nasty cough, said,

"Your mother hated the world and everyone in it."

True enough.

I asked,

"But why did you spend so much time with her?"

He looked up at the ceiling, which was discolored from the years when people smoked, said,

"The oldest reason in the book."

"To give her comfort."

"For money."

I could have lashed him for taking sorely needed cash from our strapped household but what was the point? He seemed to be in a hell that was hot enough already. I had stoked plenty of fires in my life. He said,

"Terrible curse to be in a job you have no faith in and the very people you are meant to serve distrust and loathe you."

Try as I might, I had no sympathy for the clergy. Even now they ruled with an arrogance that was breathtaking. I said,

"So resign, stop whining, do something."

He laughed, almost amused, asked,

"And what pray would I do? Where would I live? I know some half-remembered theology and some half-arsed Latin, not exactly cutting-edge stuff."

I reached for my coat, there is only so much self-pity you can endure. I said,

"I'd like to say it's been a blast."

He looked at me, asked,

"How are you fixed?"

I wanted to scream, being touched by a priest, so many ironies therein. I said,

"Keeping the tradition alive are you? Tap the son now?"

He near whispered,
"Couple hundred is all."
Jesus and his mother.
At the bar, I laid a twenty on the counter, said to the
guy,
"Buy him another."
I didn't look back.

"They buried him deep. Again."
(Joe R. Lansdale, *The Return*)

Park was cruising in his aunt's BMW, relishing the feel and control of the car. It was like the rules of language, rewarded proper usage. He headed out toward the bay and, as he cleared the promenade, opened her up, letting the speed rise to eighty.

Chirp . . . the beep of the siren and he saw the Guard car in his mirror. Considered giving them a run but sighed and slowed, pulled into the verge.

Waited.

Watched as Sergeant Ridge sauntered toward him, arrogance in all her bearing. This woman was becoming a serious nuisance, like an apostrophe in all the wrong places. She signaled for him to roll down the window, said,

"License and registration."

He took a deep breath, letters spun and whirled before his eyes. He had to push down the compulsion to grab her and smash her head against the road. He said,

"It is my aunt's vehicle. I, alas, don't have my own license with me."

She gave a hollow laugh, said,

"Now that is too bad. Get out of the car."
Waited a beat,
Then added,
"Sir?"
He got out slowly, a cloud of letters dancing before his eyes

K H e

   i

r   ll

He stared at the formation and Ridge took a step back, not liking the expression of fascination on his face.

He cupped his hands and arranged the letters.

Exhaled as they danced, whirled, then formed,

Kill

Her.

He said,

"Not yet."

Ridge put her hand on the baton fastened to her tunic, asked,

"Are you all right, sir?"

He gave her a beatific smile, said,

"Completely."

She composed herself, shaken more than she wanted to admit, said,

"As you have no license, I'm afraid I will have to forbid you from driving this vehicle. I could bring you to the station but your lawyer would throw a fit."

Park stared at her, a dreamy slant to his eyes, said,

"You are right about that."

She asked,

234

"What?"

"Being afraid."

Sergeant Ridge was more rattled by Park than by anyone else in a long time. For a Guard, threats were a daily occurrence. You took note of them without letting them run riot. You were supposed to log the threat and time at the station lest, God forbid, you got hurt. That way they had not only evidence but a written record.

She didn't log it.

There was something so radically different about this case. It kept her off balance and she had the uneasy feeling that Park was so off the radar that normal rules didn't apply. Back at her apartment, she tried to relax, had a glass of white wine, but her taste ran to something with more bite. She'd been born and raised in the Gaeltacht, the Irish-speaking part of Connemara. Wine was viewed as penance, what you had when you gave up drinking for Lent.

Jack Taylor had introduced her to the joy of books and had been guiding her in the canon of crime writers. Had said,

"You can't go wrong with James Lee Burke."

She put the latest Burke aside, and paced her living room.

Taylor.

AWOL.

Again.

Word was that he'd gone on a mighty skite. Few could lash the booze like him. Her feelings toward him veered from outright hatred to an affection she couldn't fathom. Their great friend, a Zen-practicing former drug dealer, had been killed and she blamed Jack's negligence for that.

Stewart.

Just to speak his name scalded her heart. She'd made a connection with him unlike any other. As the modern idiom put it,

He got her.

There was a lot to get. A gay woman in the Guards. Didn't come much more difficult than that. Add her habitual simmering anger and she made a hard person to befriend. She had so many defenses and buttresses that she no longer even knew what she was so fucking angry about.

He cut through all that.

By kindness.

The only other man who'd been kind in her life was her dad. He had that basic integrity that is so rare as to be mistaken for altruism. Sad now as she recalled the expression on her father's face when she announced she was joining the Guards. He'd flexed his fingers, a sure indicator, with him, of being both vexed and bitterly disappointed. He said, and worse, said very quietly,

"I'd prefer you to be a fucking nun than a Guard."

Later, when he'd heard she was coming out as gay, he'd asked,

"Why do you have to tell the world?"

Indeed.

She, to her shame now, had lectured him on honesty. Jesus.

He had very little, as James Lee Burke characters might have said,

"Book learning."

But he could rise to near elegance when he was moved. He said with infinite sadness,

"There are valid reasons almost for poverty but none for ignorance."

Rigid even then, she'd pushed,

"What does that even mean?"

He had looked her full in the face, said,

"True poverty is a dedicated selfishness disguised as polished principle."

Her mother had said,

"Your father will come round."

She was wrong.

At his funeral, Ridge, still seeking endorsement, had whined to her mother,

"I was a disappointment to him."

Never, ever seek false endorsement from fierce Irishwomen. They won't tell you what you want, they will tell you what they think, and it is never pretty. She answered simply,

"You were."

Live with that.

Later, after her mother had given his clothes to St. Vincent de Paul, she said to Ridge,

"You may want his rosary beads?"

Not really.

I mean, WTF?

She said,

"I would love that."

They had been blessed by one of the popes or indeed many of them and had touched the hem of Padre Pio, thus acquiring a slight aroma of roses. Her mother relayed all this with a very tiny note of skepticism, as in hedging her eternal bets.

As Irishwomen are expert at.

The beads were truly beautiful, a heavy gold cross and white ivory links. She said,

"Try not to think of them as handcuffs."

Thus scoring many points with one simple utterance. They were on the small table by Ridge's bed until one of her lovers asked they be put away as they induced guilt.

Surely the whole point.

Ridge was unable to settle. She replayed the arrest of Park so many times that she could actually see the expression on his face, a blend of arrogance and a surprising kind of naïveté. Later, she'd gone back to the house as the crew collected anything that might be used in evidence. They desperately needed this to be a sure thing.

On a bookshelf was just about every volume on grammar ever published. The books seemed obscure and impenetrable to her. Irish was her first language and English literally the language of work. She was ignorant in the workings of both and cared less.

She'd run her hand along the middle shelf and a sheet of paper fell out. She'd scanned it and, with a jolt, felt it could be vital. But she didn't trust her male colleagues to credit her with this and needed to think on it further. She had stuffed it into her jacket and now unfolded it, read anew.

From
The Serpent Papers
By
Jessica Cornwell.
Like this:

. . .

A groans like dried blood
R regal, dark
D as indigo
I makes a bright light
E is the color yellow

She muttered,
"The shite does this mean?"
She could imagine producing this in court and the lawyer annihilating her. Once upon a time, she could have shown this to Jack and he would have made some sense of it. She felt more alone than ever and then shook herself. Fixed her face, did her hair, put on a white silk T she'd been saving
For what?
There were no more special occasions. Grabbed her short leather jacket, black with studs to get the dyke vibe out there. And for some reason, that sailed the bitch Emily into her head.
Jack seemed completely smitten with the idea of the woman.

Ridge felt that Emily had perfected the Devil's greatest trick, persuading the world he didn't exist. Emily seemed to live large in Jack's imagination.

Freudian thought?

"What-the-fuck-ever,"

She muttered.

Managed to block that cow out of her mind and head out. The night was young and full of hopeful peril.

"I drink too much, I smoke too much,
I gamble too much, I am too much."
(Eddie "Fitz" Fitzgerald, in *Cracker*)

Everything about Pat Maloney was big.

His ego

His car

His girth

But especially his mouth.

He ordered a pint like this:

"Do me a Black."

A man beside him said,

"Tut, tut, surely you mean, may I have?"

Pat only glanced at him, a puny bollix, but then most seemed simply tiny. He said,

"Fuck off before I land me shoe in yer hole."

The man gave what might have been a delighted giggle, said,

"Oh, how you trample on the sacred ground."

Pat was distracted by his mobile and began one of those all too common exchanges of loudness and bravado. He sank most of his pint during this tirade of ostentation. When he finished, the annoying guy had disappeared. After a feed of drink Pat developed that drinker's lust for fast food. It had to be greasy, a caloric riot.

He settled for Supermac's, though greasy wasn't their forte. Their pièce de résistance was curried chips, sprinkled with melted cheese and very, very large. He ordered an extra-large Dr Pepper and said to the girl when his food arrived, as he handed her a five-euro note,

"Keep the change, darling."

There was no change unless you consider two cents that. Outside he savaged the chips, cheese running down his shirt, the wife would clean it — it was her job. He dropped the packaging, all messy and leaking, right beside a litter bin.

Then headed into the nearby alley to urinate.

As he let flow, he emitted a huge belch and thought,

"Life is fucking mighty."

A voice said,

"According to goddess Truss, it is generally accepted that familiar contractions such as bus (omnibus) no longer require apostrophes."

Then his head was crushed by a ferocious blow to the skull.

"I have no idea where this will lead us, but I have a definite feeling it will be a place both wonderful and strange."
(Dale Cooper, in *Twin Peaks*)

I got back to Galway — not a month later but nigh on two. Booze costs you time as well as just about everything else. Last lingering days in London, what I most spent my time at, apart from attempting to beat hangovers and fret about dwindling money, was, get this,

Watching YouTube.

One clip.

Titled "Wet Dog."

Featured a Brussels griffon pup who was as weird and wretched as I felt. He was having what seemed to be a very human nervous breakdown and was flat-out funny and touching. Of course it reminded me of my pup, Storm, and how he was. I'm not claiming I returned because of him but it was in the mix. The only consolation was I missed Christmas and New Year shabby resolutions. If you want the very rock bottom of festivities, in all its naked misery and squalor, try a bedsit in Camden Town.

During my final London weeks, I'd watched *Wolf Hall* and marveled at the absolute stillness of Mark Rylance as Thomas Cromwell. In an era of all things

Kardashian, it was quite astonishing to see such major talent and with such little movement. In some ways, I'd have killed for stillness and perhaps only being killed would still me.

Still.

"Come late the murder . . . come.
Flee the black." (The White Buffalo)

Before I left London, I had some odd, not to mention almost mystical, encounters. Perhaps it was simply the befuddlement of drink or too much postponed grief but I had headed to Leicester Square to do an old-fashioned act. Some inverted homage to the generations of Irish who took the cattle boats to the UK. Never to return, swallowed up in Kilburn, on damp building sites, in Kentish Town and dead pubs and Cricklewood and death sentence boardinghouses, six to a shitty room.

To book passage home on the ferry.

No online booking, just the physical action of getting a ticket over the counter, one way only. The music of De Danann and the Leicester Square Odeon; it was showing *Fifty Shades of Grey*.

Nostalgia through utter nonsense.

A homeless man looked at me beseechingly, utterly silent.

I put a tenner in the guy's cap and he went,
"Hey?"

I turned back and looked at him. He had the shadowed face of the wretched but a beatific smile, said,

"Landau dumping, a strange phenomenon that occurs as a consequence of the energy exchange between electromagnetic waves and gases in a state of plasma."

With Google, later, I would find this was part of *Birth of a Theorem* by Cédric Villani, the punk rock mathematician.

No, me neither.

I said,

"You what?"

He smiled, said,

"Or, as O'Casey put it, the whole world is in a state of chassis."

The night before I took the boat, I watched a horror movie.

Mad, eh?

In my heightened state, you would think it was the last thing I'd want to see. A debut by an Australian woman titled

The Babadook.

A scary simple masterpiece. Oh, yeah, a dog got killed in it. Of course. Left me even jumpier than I was. Next day, I packed my meager belongings: a leather coat I got on Camden Lock; books, of course; a silver flask with Jay and Guinness; and no hope in my heart. In my mind was Ed Sheeran with

"Make It Rain."

As I boarded the ferry at Holyhead after an arduous train ride from Euston, ahead of me in the line were a father and son. The boy was maybe eight or so and woebegone. The man, slight, with that fading weak

252

blond hair, stooped gait, and air of furtiveness. The boy caught my eye and smiled. I didn't.

I was all out of cordiality.

As we pulled out of the dock, I went up on deck and stared at the retreating English coastline. I threw a bent penny over the side and wished

For . . .

Nothing.

I was sitting in the ship's lounge, which was packed. Seemed people still liked to travel this way and of course it was convenient for traveling with children. I was rereading David Gates's *Jernigan*. Class act. Alongside the novel *Stoner*, it reaffirmed the power of narrative and especially the art of desperation. It sang to me the dark melodies of

Loss

The broken

The wounded

Indeed.

Like holding a mirror up to my battered life.

Heard

"Mind if we take this seat?"

The man and boy.

I said,

"Sure."

I noticed the boy sat absolutely still, like a tiny Thomas Cromwell. The father, by contrast, was a study in fidgeting. He checked his pockets, pushed his fingers through his thinning hair, checked his phone, then looked around like a bird of prey or a trapped one. Finally he leaned toward me, asked,

"I'm terribly sorry to bother you but would you mind watching Daniel while I grab a pint?"

I gave him a cold look, said,

"Make it snappy."

I swear the boy nearly smiled. The man took it like the lash it was but rallied, said,

"Aye aye, skipper."

And fucked off.

I tried to get back to the book but was aware the boy was staring intently at me, I went,

"Was there something?"

He had those huge saucer eyes, blue and grave. He asked,

"Do you think, I'm, like, weird?"

Duh.

I don't know how to talk to kids. I mean, I can talk to people — well, some, anyway, and give me a few pints, I'd talk to the pope. I can talk to dogs and that's no hardship, they are busy loving you regardless, even if you talk shite. Kids though,

Phew-oh.

I answered,

"Why would you think that?"

He thought about that, then,

"I don't have any friends."

Me neither. I said,

"Well, you're young and lots of time."

Fucking wisdom of the ages from me. He asked,

"Are you very, like, old?"

Fuck.

Then before I could lie my way around that, he said,

"My dad is sick."

Okay.

I asked,

"From what?"

"Drink."

I racked my remaining brain cells and got this gem:

"How about Xbox, you play those?"

"No."

I looked around desperately for his father, realized I had a slight sheen of sweat on my brow, said,

"I'm sure you have a wonderful life ahead of you."

He stared at me in utter derision, then said,

"Fuck me."

Okay . . .

He began to recite in his very proper English accent,

. . . *Give up Paris*

You will never create anything

By reading Racine

He pronounced Racine like Rancid.

Continued,

. . . *and Arthur Symons will always*

Be

A better critic of French Literature.

He took a deep childlike breath, then,

. . . *Go to the Aran Islands,*

Live there as if you were one of the people themselves

Express a life that has never found expression.

He took a swig of a large bottle of Dr Pepper, asked,

"Do you know who wrote that?"

"I don't."

"Yeats."

I had nothing to add to this and he said,

"Me and him are going to live on the Aran Islands."

Oddly, he referred to his dad as *him*. Said *him* came back, three sheets to a whiskeyed wind, asked,

"You like Robbie Coltrane?"

Before I could answer this nonsense, he added,

"They have a betting shop on board."

Just what the world needs.

His face had that barroom tan, the high color you get when you fast swallow the drinks and the booze suffuses your cheeks with a false sheen of health. And he had that limited bonhomie that is as intense as it is short-lived. I said,

"I'm Jack Taylor and I've already met Daniel."

He shot the boy a warning glance, as in,

"Shut your fucking mouth."

He said,

Turning,

"So poking your nose in my affairs already."

Coming hard arse at me, it's where I live, what I love. I snapped,

"Depends on what you've got to hide."

His eyes flashed, rage pushing to be let out. I could help there. I put out my hand, the mutilated fingers on full show, gritted,

"So, your name?"

He gave a shrill laugh, well, more of a giggle, said,

"Good Lord, you sound like a cop."

Daniel blurted,

"He's not my father."

Pause.

Now we had us a whole other interesting game of hurling. Instinctively he raised his fist and I said, real quiet,

"Touch the boy and I will fuck you over the side."

Needless to say, this was something of a conversation killer. The guy blurted,

"No need to get all het up."

I asked, steel leaking all over my tone,

"What are you to the boy?"

Maybe I read it wrong but the boy seemed to be suppressing a smile. The guy offered his hand, said,

"We seem to be off on the wrong foot. I'm Stanley Reed, and I'm the boy's uncle."

In pedophile talk, *uncle* has a whole other connotation, and the guy suddenly realized that, tried,

"The boy's mum is poorly and I'm taking him for a bit of a break to the Aran Islands."

I stood up and he reached for my arm, pleaded,

"Please give me a minute,"

Looked at Daniel, added,

"Away from the boy."

We moved out to a corridor but it was jammed. Between the cinemas, bowling, bingo, the place was a mini mall. We headed into the men's room and

He started,

"You like hookers and margaritas?"

WTF?

Then,

"Who doesn't, right? My treat?"
I asked,
"What the fuck is wrong with you? You think I want to go . . ."
Reached for the description,
"Do you want to party?"
Added,
"With you?"
He sighed, said,
"Guess not."
Then sucker-punched me in the gut; it hurt.

As I bent over, he grabbed my hair, used his knee to break my nose, let me fall, and did a rapid series of vicious kicks to my head and face. In my head, Elton John was unspooling.

"I can see Daniel waving good-bye."
Reed bent down, whispered in my ear,
"I paid good money for that little *cunt*, and you know what, hotshot? He is nearly too old for my taste already."
Paused.
"How time flies when you are fucking . . ."
Another pause.
". . . Sweetness."

"An event may be considered decisive when it utterly destabilizes your life. This event which sends a jolt of electricity through your nervous system is readily distinguishable from life's other misfortunes because it has a particular force, a specific density; as soon as it occurs, you realize that it will have overwhelming consequences, that what is happening in your life is irreparable."
(Pierre Lemaitre, *Camille*)

Lapsing into a Comma
(Bill Walsh)

They used to say that you came to a full stop when you died. I've had many beatings in my time, with

Hurleys

Steel-capped boots (courtesy of two rogue Guards)

Baseball bats

Blunt instruments of various hues, including whiskey bottles and KA-BARs.

But this hiding in the toilet of the ferry was close to being the worst.

In the movies, the hero takes a beat-down, he rises with designer bruises and gung ho attitude. They don't show you soiling yourself to add shame to the hurt. Lying there, in piss and blood, you do your damnedest not to cry.

Doesn't work.

This blubbering mess of myself was airlifted to the Beaumont hospital. And another month lost as I rallied, relapsed, suffered, and withered. But they persevered and a few days before my release Sergeant Ridge traveled all the way from Galway to interrogate me.

Sweet girl.

★　★　★

Ridge looked tired and old. She stood at the end of my bed, disapproval writ large and largest. As I struggled to sit upright and face the shitstorm, the lyrics of Nine Inch Nails, "Somewhat Damaged," riffed in my head. I asked,

"What kept you?"

She shook her head, said,

"Always the mouth."

I'd have murdered somebody for a drink, a cig, asked,

"You bring any tidings of good cheer, or refreshments?"

Her face was locked in distaste, she was not going to bend an inch. Said,

"You disappear. For months, not even your wacko bitch friend, the Emily cow, knew where you were. Couldn't find her or even a trace of her, as if she was a figment of your deranged imagination.

"I've been told you were paid by Parker Wilson's niece to prove his innocence. I'm simply here to see if you have any information to move the whole mess forward, though from your appearance I'd guess it was just your usual piss-up, disguised as an investigation."

The guy on the ferry beat me up professionally. Now Ridge was going to beat me down with guilt. I said,

"There's a man, a pedophile, traveling with a young boy, heading I think for the Aran Islands. You need to find them."

She sighed, a sigh my cursed mother would have owned, said,

262

"And I'm your messenger boy? Am I to gather this guy beat the holy crap out of you?"

I tried,

"Put your personal feelings for me aside. A boy is in serious danger."

She nearly smiled, a smile of utter joylessness, said,

"I put everything about you aside a long time ago."

We traded a few more insults but, truly, they were halfhearted, we had kind of lost the ability to really wound each other after Stewart died. I gave her the description of the man and boy, asked,

"How is the case on the grammar guy progressing?"

She was going to ignore that but veered, said,

"Another murder and we still can't pin it on him."

She took out a notebook, wrote down the details of the man and boy, said,

"I'll do background on the man, see if we get a red flag."

I wanted to say thank you but knew she'd blow that down so settled for,

"Well, mind yourself."

Lame as fuck but in Ireland we say it when we don't really want to go with

"Go fuck yourself."

She did that long searching look, the one that implies,

"Surely there is something of merit in you . . ."

But

"Fucked if I can see it."

She said,

"No point, Jack, in wishing you luck, you are so far out on borrowed time, it's beyond comprehension."

And she was gone.

Leaving a blank space that whispered,

"All is ashes."

The nurse came in, did the annoying fluffing pillows gig, said,

"I thought you were going to be arrested."

I settled down in the bed, said,

"Not too late."

She slammed a thermometer into my mouth, said,

"You need to get a positive attitude."

Yes, that was really what was missing with my life.

" 'Sudan won't be happy with you,' she said. 'You're abnormal. You're sick in the head. I tried. God knows I tried.' She didn't say what she had tried. Before leaving, as she passed in front of Terrier, she raised herself up on tiptoe and spit clumsily in his face."
(Jean-Patrick Manchette, *The Prone Gunman — La position du tireur couché*)

Emily was raising a frozen margarita to her lips, seated in the bar of the newest cocktail club off Shop Street. Time back, this had been a lap dancing club but the Church, with its dwindling power, managed to get the place closed. Cocktail bars weren't really a Galway thing but some poor fool forever kept trying. The locals gave it, tops, a month before it shut. Meanwhile, it was thriving, if briefly.

Doc came storming in, dressed in what ex-army guys thought of as casual. Cords, topped off with the fucked worn wax jackets, like a royal who wandered off from a pheasant shoot.

Took him a minute to find his bearings. He looked like someone who'd stumbled into the wrong scene in the wrong movie. Then he saw her, glared, and marched over. She raised her glass in mock salute.

He plunged,

"Where the hell have you been? Three days you don't come home?"

She took a long hit of the margarita, then spoke very quietly.

"Home? Are you seriously calling the rabbit hole you have . . ."

Pause.

"Home?"

Got him.

Good.

Before he could stammer a reply, she said,

"I was using you as a way to be close to Jack and, hey, guess what, it didn't, like, work."

He moved to sit down, weakness hurling at his knees, and she hissed in that same lethal quiet tone,

"Don't sit."

He had served two terms in NI, did a stint in Bosnia, and very little fazed him anymore but now he was, well, fucked. He tried,

"What am I supposed to do, darling?"

She seemed to be seriously contemplating this, then,

"Hop on over there, get me another one of these babes."

He looked forlornly toward the bar and she added,

"One more thing, macchiato."

"Yes?"

"Don't ever call me darling again."

Tail between your legs. Doc had heard it many times but now knew what it truly felt like. He stood outside the bar, no idea where to go, when he heard,

"Doc. Is it Doc?"

The woman seemed vaguely familiar and, like most people in this damned city, in some way connected to Taylor. She said,

"I'm Sergeant Ridge. We met briefly last year."

He didn't remember and could care less. He said,

"Shouldn't you be off catching the grammar lunatic?"

She gave a tight forced smile, said,

"I see being friends with Mr. Taylor has rubbed off on your attitude."

He looked up at the sky and, as always, it seemed on the verge of storm, and how fucking fitting that was. He said,

"Unless you wanted me for anything, why don't you just, in the idiom of this lovely town, fuck right off?"

Ridge watched him slump away. She had heard he'd been in the army but any trace of military bearing seemed to have been sucked right out of him. One thing she knew from being a Guard, a man looks that downbeat, there is usually a woman involved. On instinct, she headed into the bar. It was her evening off but maybe she could combine a few cocktails and work. Saw Emily immediately. All the energy in the room seemed to gravitate toward her. She thought,

"Bloody bitch."

With an enigmatic smile, Emily watched her approach. As Ridge reached for a seat, she said,

"Don't join me."

Ridge smiled. Nothing she liked better than a confrontation.

She sat.

Emily studied her, said,

"See the clothes budget is a bit stretched, or is that a gay thing? You know, looking cheap?"

Ridge signaled a waiter, ordered a rum and Coke. The waitress protested,

"We have a full range of cocktails, I could provide the menu . . ."

Ridge didn't even look at her, said,

"Just get the bloody drink."

Emily curled up into herself, not from defense but from utter delight, said,

"Oh, that is so forceful. I'm guessing you're the bull dyke in the gig."

Ridge continued to watch her, but Emily didn't blink, which gained a tiny measure of grudging respect. She said,

"In your somewhat colorful history and indeed brief one, you have managed to be around the scene of three murders."

Emily put her glass on the table, said,

"Four."

Ridge's drink came and the waitress asked,

"Ice?"

Ridge with a tight smile said,

"No need, the atmosphere here is more than arctic."

Then she took a slow sip of the drink, savored, said,

"Your friend Taylor has surfaced."

Emily tried to mask her surprise and Ridge continued,

"Ah, so something you didn't know."

Emily suppressed the urge to inquire and stayed immobile. Her heart was pounding, damn it. Ridge let her stew for a bit, then,

"He is in hospital and it crossed my mind that maybe you put him there."

Emily hid her distress and continued to work on her drink. Ridge switched tracks, said,

"Your paper trail is interesting, if not yet downright criminal, but I have the feeling you are on the verge of serious fuckup."

Pause.

"And I will so enjoy that moment, the moment you are completely done."

Emily waited a full five minutes and few things are longer than minutes when you are playing verbal chess, said,

"I have to wonder if your obsession with me is professional or if it's some kind of gay twisted mind-fuck?"

Ridge kept her cool, surprising even herself, said,

"I do like a bad girl but no one likes a sick cow."

Stood, felt she had gotten the last word, was near the door when Emily said, very quietly,

"Blowback's a bitch."

"If I got rid of my demons, I'd lose my angels." (Tennessee Williams)

"On the page, punctuation performs its grammatical function, but in the mind of the reader it does more than that. It tells the reader how to hum the tune." (Lynne Truss, *Eats, Shoots & Leaves*)

I woke, the meeting between Ridge and Emily so real in my mind it was hard to credit it was but a dream.

Jesus, when did dreams have such accurate, if loaded, narrative and dialogue? I could taste the margarita on my tongue but, dream notwithstanding, I was glad that Doc got a shoe in his arse, even if wish fulfillment was all it was.

Some people are haunted by memories; me, it's priests. Can't seem to shake them. The day before I was released from hospital, I was sitting up in bed, reading,

A Rumor of Ghosts.

Three sisters who decide to commit suicide on the same night. Hooked me by the line,

"First thing you need to know about our family is we're quitters."

I was engrossed in this when a shadow fell across the bed, looked up to see a priest. He was dressed clerical casual. Black V-neck sweater, black slacks, and tiny gold cross on a chain around his neck. Discreet if not showy. He had that new humble shit-eating smile they've adopted since they went on the endangered list. He opened,

"Hope I'm not disturbing you."

He wasn't . . . hoping. Just trotting out the line in mock servitude. I said,

"The clergy have been disturbing us for centuries so why worry?"

He gave a tentative smile, wanted to look back to gauge the distance to the door. He said,

"You're Catholic."

Infuriating me. I snapped,

"What gave that away, the guilt, the fucked-up look?"

Staggered him, the venom almost tangible in the very air. He rallied, as they do, centuries of *making this shit up as you go* training kicking in. He said,

"The miraculous medal might have been a clue?"

I nearly smiled, said,

"Madonna has seven of them and not even her taste could be described as catholic."

He went with,

"Touché."

He held out his hand, said,

"I'm Paul."

He near recoiled at the sight of my mutilated fingers. Normally I keep them well disguised but lately I was real bad at hiding anything. I shook his hand and felt a slight tremor, and thought,

"Ah, a drinker."

Explained the high color. I said,

"Jack Taylor."

Then I began to get out of bed, said,

"Jesus, don't just stand there, help me."

He didn't, asked,

"You want to go to the bathroom?"

"Fuck no. I want to get a few pints in before they start the rigmarole of discharging me."

Took me a time to get dressed and he asked,

"Is it wise? I mean, to leave the hospital?"

I gave my bitter laugh, more in use these days, said,

"Wise? Fuck, if I were wise I'd have bought shares in Irish Water."

I felt a spasm of weakness and leaned on the jamb of the door to get right, said,

"I might for the first time in my life have to lean on the clergy."

He took my arm and asked,

"You want me to assist you to a pub?"

"I want you to buy me a few drinks and tell me the nature of evil."

I am sure we made a bizarre pair, a wounded beaten man, being aided reluctantly by a priest. Like all Irish hospitals, it was but a rosary away from the pub.

There's a different vibe from Galway pubs. You feel they don't want you but a sly cunning keeps them from saying so. No wonder the poet Patrick Kavanagh felt so comfortable in them. We got seated, near the back, at my choosing, the priest observing,

"You need to watch your back?"

I snarled,

"If I did I wouldn't be with you."

Landed.

He said,

"You are a very bitter, cynical man."

"Thank you."

I ordered a pint and Jay, him a Britvic orange. I said,

"Man up, have a fucking drink. You're paying, might as well get a blast out of it."

He took a gin and tonic and seemed relieved to have the decision made for him, judging by the way he gulped it. I didn't comment, asked,

"So you're on the hospital beat?"

He did the *only exist to serve* gig, half slit eyes and sad smile, or it could simply have been the gin. He said,

"Any small comfort we can provide."

I drained my glass, asked,

"Where is the Church on evil these days? Still proclaiming that God's ways are too mysterious to fathom?"

He made a show of checking his watch, a nice Tissot — not much poverty there — then,

"I see all of human weakness, foibles, cruelty, greed played out on a smaller stage every day."

Deep.

I pushed, disbelief leaking over my words,

"In the hospital?"

He nearly smiled, said,

"*Judge Judy.*"

I kind of liked him a bit better for that. He checked his watch again. I said,

"Hey, don't let me keep you from anything."

He sighed, sounding a lot like my dead mother who had, dare I say,

. . . *the mother of sighs.*

She had that fake world-weary sucker nailed. He said,

278

"I have confessions and need to prepare."

I gave him my concrete stare, said,

"I was under the impression it was now the *sacrament of reconciliation*, but maybe you're not into that whole reconciliation shite?"

He took a rosary out of his pocket, a fine object, heavy silver cross, blue beads that caught the light. He said,

"This was blessed in Guadalupe."

I sneered. Blame the fast Jay, said,

"Ah, the Madonna of the cartels."

He shook his head, muttered,

"You really are the most trying man."

Then he handed me the beads, I didn't do the dance of . . . *Oh, no, I couldn't possibly*,

I put them around my neck figuring I could use all the help I could get, Mexican or otherwise. I asked,

"I look like Bono?"

"You mean spiritual?"

"No, asshole."

"She's so beautiful. If there weren't a junkie in my room, shitting and retching and hurling, it'd be just like *Pride and Prejudice*." (Joshua Braff, *Peep Show*)

Park Wilson was yet again being interviewed by the Guards. They knew they had no concrete evidence but no harm in trying. The rattle-the-cage method. The only one rattled was Park's aunt, Sarah. She had immediately called the lawyer, who quite crossly snapped,

"Say nothing, keep saying nothing."

Then, practicing his own advice, hung up.

Sarah, getting right in Sergeant Ridge's face, implored,

"Can you please stop this harassment?"

Ridge gave a vaguely tolerant smile.

"Inquiries must be followed."

Sarah, throwing up her hands, turned to Park, who was sitting peacefully in an armchair, demanded,

"Park, say something!"

He looked at Ridge, said,

"Beware of *heard* and sounds like *bird*

. . . And *dead;* it's said like *bed*, not *bead*."

Ridge, dressed in full sergeant's regalia and with two brutes of Garda, had decided she was going to get a result. She got right in Park's face. He seemed to be actually looking at a point beyond her head. She pushed,

"Do you get the effect you're having on your poor aunt?"

His head snapped back and he near spat,

"*Effect?*"

. . . long withering pause.

"Affect?"

"*Affect* is a verb, *effect* is a noun, and you would do well to remember that, woman."

Ridge was near speechless, tried,

"What?"

Park gave her a blissful smile, said,

"A cat has claws at the end of its paws.

. . . A comma's a pause at the end of a clause."

Ridge threw up her hands in exasperation, said,

"You are required to report to the Guards station every Thursday morning. Failure to do so will entail immediate revocation of your bail."

He continued to smile at her, muttering now about dropped subjunctives. She gave the aunt a hard look and signaled to the Guards they were done.

For now.

Outside she let loose a string of obscenities. The Guard nearest her observed,

"The guy is a raving lunatic."

She agreed that might be so but he was a particularly sly one. The other Guard asked,

"So how are we going to catch him?"

Ridge told the truth.

"I have no fucking idea."

The Guard thought that was choice language for a lady but kept that thought to himself.

"The Detective thinks he is investigating a murder. But truly he is investigating something else, something he cannot grasp hold of directly. Satisfaction will be rare. Uncertainty will be your natural state. Sources will always elude you. The detective will always circle around what he wants, never seeing it whole. We go on NOT despite this. We go on because of it."
(Sara Gran, *Claire DeWitt and the City of the Dead*)

Back to my hometown.

And back I came, not in glory or richness. The first person I ran into went,

"I thought you were dead!"

Uh-huh.

I went to my apartment and opened all the windows, like a sign proclaiming,

"Come all ye burglars and thieves."

I was deeply conscious of the pup not being there. His treats and toys lay on the floor like abandoned prayer, joyless and futile. Opened the wardrobe to find

Brand-new Donegal tweed jacket with a note:

. . . If you ever come home

. . . Emily the deserted.

Tried on the jacket and it fitted like found money. Had patches on the elbows, giving me that worn John Cheever vibe, as if I were some underpaid elderly professor of lit at a hole-in-the-wall second-grade college. The kind of place where grammar still mattered.

And thinking of grammar . . .

My current client, the aunt of the alleged Grammarian, would be anxious to see what the hell I had done with her money. I don't think a sabbatical had been her intention.

My first call was to the small house Maeve lived in. She was one of the nuns on the order's *outreach program*.

Meaning, she lived outside the convent grounds to maintain a link to the people. The program had chosen well. Maeve was a real person, subject to fits of anger, joy, annoyance, and not afraid to show you. Most nuns kept all that good shit bottled up and hidden. As soon as I knocked on her door, I could hear the pup go wild. Short-term memory is ascribed to dogs. My pup hadn't got the memo. The door opened and he was all over me.

Broke my heart anew.

Maeve said,

"I wondered if he would remember you and there's the answer."

Maeve gave the whole nun story some credibility. If love is, as they say,

"*the selfless consideration for the welfare of another person*"

Then she was love in a habit. Of course to blend in she wore civilian clothes mostly but she retained the air of someone who viewed the world from beneath a cowl. I was curious and asked,

"Did you always, you know, want to be, like, a nun?"

Hating myself for adding the qualifier *like*. The riff of the newly Americanized Irish youth. She massaged the pup's ear as she considered her answer, then,

"I wanted to be a dancer."

WTF?

I said,

"Seriously?"

She laughed.

"No, I won lots of medals for Irish dancing but this was in the days before Michael Flatley and there was no career in that world. I went into the convent because I was scared of life."

Fuck, how many people are going to fess up to that? I asked,

"And now, are you fearless?"

She gave a lovely laugh, the kind that makes you briefly glad to be part of the human race. She said,

"I just learned what to be afraid of and, more importantly, how to avoid it."

I didn't believe most of that but I liked her so I let it slide.

I asked,

"Could I bring you for dinner?"

Good heavens, she blushed. I'm not sure where on a bucket list a blushing nun would merit but it is a rush. She said,

"Oh, Lord, I've never been invited anywhere unless you count the Irish stew competition in Loughrea."

In the pup's minimalist vocabulary there are some key words and dinner is right up there. He shook himself and bounced off a wall. In canine, that is delight, I think. She was all bothered, said,

"I don't know what to say."

"Say yes."

She did.

We went to the Park Hotel, it has a rep for genteel. I figured an egg and fast bacon caff wasn't really the speed for a nun. We had left the pup with ample treats but he still whined. Dogs only know from,

"You're present or you're not."

Bit like a tax audit.

Maeve ordered whiting with lemon garnish and lots of, her word,

"Chips."

I identified with the childlike delight in having real chips all for your own self. Coaxed her into a glass of white wine and I stayed relatively good if you count a bottle of Bud as that. I ordered steak, burned to a damn cinder, for my own good self. As we had left her home, she had hefted a large bag, more like a satchel, and I asked,

"Your rosary?"

I come from the generation where nuns wore chain-like beads around their waists. Less for devotion than whacking. Now she reached in there and produced a blue volume, said,

"I want to give you this, you being a man of books and . . ."

She hesitated,

"Um . . . an inclination for drink."

Just about the politest form of being called a rummy. It was *The Big Book of Alcoholics Anonymous*. The whole mood just upped and fucked right off.

I limped out with,

"Oh."

Deep, huh?

She said,

"My sister died from alcoholism and I found this among her things."

The devil was in me to sneer,

"Didn't do her a whole load of good, right?"

But managed to blow that off, went,

"You don't exactly see me falling down, Sister."

And okay, so maybe a tiny wee hint of hard leaked over my tone. She reached over, touched my hand, and that hurt me, in ways I can't even begin to articulate. She said,

"I have seen you fall, Jack."

Ah, fuck it, why'd she have to add my name?

The food came like a belated Seventh Cavalry and I said,

"Looks good."

I think I meant the food. She unfolded her napkin in that facile, fluent way that nuns have, all biz and industry. She said, very quietly,

"There is a line in that book that says . . ."

Pause.

". . . *unless the alcoholic finds a spiritual solution.*"

I shook my head, picked up my fork, and moved my food around the plate, like the very last line in a very bad poem. She got it, tried,

"I have offended you, Jack."

Ah, sweet Jesus.

I said,

"No offense, Sister, but you don't really know me well enough to do that."

Of all the things that might have come down the pike after that exchange, the very last thing I would have called

Was

. . . tears.

A tiny tear sneaked out of her left eye and slowly trailed down her unlined cheek and hit the plate with the softest ping. My heart tore at its shredded remnants.

There must be a special circle of hell for those who make one of the very few decent nuns weep. I offered my napkin and pleaded,

"Please don't."

She dabbed daintily at the cheek and whispered,

"I have always been too soft. Reverend Mother said I was a pathetic excuse for one of God's soldiers."

It burst out of me.

"The bad bitch."

And she laughed.

Oh, thank Christ. The waitress came over, asking,

"Is everything all right?"

I said,

"Two shots of Jameson."

Maeve stared at the Jay when it came, said,

"I must confess . . ."

Like the opening of the song

"Finished."

"I've never tasted whiskey."

Oh, come on.

I raised my glass, clinked hers, said,

"Slainte amach."

The shot hit her like a very bad novena, fast and nasty. She gulped, then,

"I could develop a taste for that."

Man, I knew what she meant, that fierce kick in the gut and head of quality hooch. Why we chase the bitch for so long. I said,

"Could I share my current case with you?"

She laughed, now quite frisky, asked,

"You have a case of this magic drink?"

Jesus.

What had I unleashed?

I said,

"No, I mean I wish but I mean the situation I am supposed to be working on now."

Mean . . . twice in one sentence, the Grammarian would kill me.

A

    N

       D

Bingo!

The solution to how to solve the case.

Sweet fucking disbelief.

Who knew?

Maybe it was hanging with the clergy, nun better, so to speak. Bring the war to him. Crash and burn language in his presence and see how he ran?

Maeve eyed my glass and burped, then,

"I have a very fat pink pig."

Hello?

Did nuns see pigs where we mere mortals saw pink elephants?

She laughed, said,

"It's a fat porcelain one and I put all my spare change in there for Enable Ireland, I call it 'The pig sings charity.'"

I knew that reference from Anthony de Mello's book Awareness.

". . . Trying to get people to change is like trying to teach a pig to sing.

All it does is annoy the pig."

Maeve then changed tack, said,

"I have holidays soon."

They get holidays?

From what?

Piety?

She saw my skepticism, smiled, said,

"I go to spend a week on the Aran Islands with my sister."

Serendipity?

I told her about my meeting on the boat with the man and boy and asked if she might inquire discreetly on them.

She was excited, said,

"I'll be like an undercover agent."

I said drily,

"Mind it doesn't become a habit."

And felt a thud in my chest and then a ferocious fit of coughing. Maeve, all concern, got me some water and the spasm passed. I paid the bill, left a hefty tip, and Maeve said,

"You are a generous man."

"Naw, I just want her to like me."

And fell on my face.

"All is changed, and for the Grammarian, changed shockingly.
Grammar, like all disciplines, is not immune to radical change."

Park Wilson never saw the brick coming. Smashed into the side of his head and, though not killing him, it shook the be-Jaysus out of his brain cells. Park had been as usual in a swirl of letters, clouds of vowels fandangoing and cartwheeling in a cacophony of verbal dexterity. A crew of kids, standing on a wall, saw him thus, engrossed and muttering to himself. The fiercest of them spat,

"Wanker"

Pulled the concrete brick loose from the wall's edge and let fly.

To his astonishment and horror, it hit the man square on the forehead, felling him instantly.

They fled.

Park twisted on the ground, the sheer impact bringing a moment of clarity unlike anything he'd ever experienced. He tried to rise but blood poured into his eyes, disorienting him. He managed to get up on one shaky knee, reached out

For help?

Letters?

Clarity?

His fingers found the said brick and he pulled it toward him, lifted it up to his face, and, momentarily wiping his eyes clear, he peered at the assault weapon, imagined he read on the side that was unbloodied

. . . a . . . e . . . i . . .

His brain started to freeze and he muttered,

"What comes after *i*?

I before *e*?

But not . . ."

What?

Holy God, what?

He fell backward, the brick slipping from his dying hand, the last vowel eluding him just as peace had eluded every decade of his insane existence.

He emitted a tiny sigh and his last breath formed, danced a little, then died on the gravel stones of the gravel path.

He died as he had lived.

Without rhyme or reason.

It was, if not a fitting epitaph, at least a grammatically correct one.

The wall the boys had been standing on was known locally as Casement's Wall. He is said to have begun building it before being arrested.

Sir Roger Casement, 1864–1916, Irish rebel, has reportedly

. . . been hanged on a comma.

At his trial, Casement had argued that the Treason Act was unpunctuated and thus not legal. Two diligent officials searched the Records Office and stated that the original document was legal. Thus the story spread that Casement had

. . . attempted to be freed by grammar.

It may have been of some scant comfort to the dead Park that a grammatical brick had done him in.

"The

        Fuckit

            List"

A variation on the so-called *bucket list*,
meaning it is compiled as if Jack Taylor
meant it, dancing as fast as he could. Driven
by a hundred forms of despair, he realized
that only grave defiance would be a response
to a literal death sentence.

A cri de coeur

        Metamorphosing

              to

                a

                 Prayer

                   in

                     the

Dying.

La mort est maintenant.

Three months in the hospital and emerged with the doctor's verdict

. . . tops?

"You have three months to live."

. . . "It is in the liver, spreading gradually to the brain.

. . . Put your affairs in order."

Or rather, in my case, disorder.

A due date focuses the mind wonderfully.

Suddenly you don't have to fret about paying the water charges. You want to weep for the pup that will be left behind.

What did I miss in the three forlorn months?

Me own self.

Ireland voting yes to same-sex marriage.

And,

On a weird connected note,

Bruce Jenner on the cover of *Vanity Fair* as a woman with the phrase

. . . "Call me Caitlyn."

Jesus wept.

Missed the Eurovision song contest.

Ah, horrors.

Missed the Grammarian being literally bricked.

I got back to my apartment and, for a few minutes, sat on the sofa in delayed shock. What I most wanted to do was simply curl up in a ball and howl. Dying!

Fuck.

Managed to stir and grab the bottle of Jay, pour a wallop, and sink it. Stood with my eyes closed until it hit my gut. Then hit it did.

Hard and wonderful. Wiped my brow and let out a slow, agonized,

. . . phew.

"Life is not about waiting for the storm to pass. It is about learning to dance in the rain."

A new storm of epic proportions was forecast and this
one, they promised,
   Was
         The Big One.
Batten down the feeble hatches. I met with my
rent-a-thug and, after a lot of haggling, got the old
revolver I wanted.
   Cost
   . . . a lot.
The guy telling me,
"You gotta pay for class."
An indication of its vintage was he could procure
only five bullets. I said,
"Should be sufficient."
Got the look and the question,
"What are you killing?"
Asked in half-jocular fashion.
I said in a similar tone,
"The past."
Back at my apartment, I dry-fired it, needed some
oil. Like my system. But it had the resounding
comforting click of the hammer dropping.

A bell tolling.

Told myself,

"Least now I never have to read Salman Rushdie."

I was on countdown to the end. The pain had upped a level and I was gut-swallowing painkillers to a limited effect.

A side effect of this intense medicine was, according to my doctor,

. . . Mild hallucinatory effect.

Mild!

I fucking beg to disagree.

A bitter cold day I stood on the rocks over Galway Bay, thought of James Lee Burke and his ghosts in the confederate mist. I saw

Tall ships

. . . Breaking on the turbulent waves.

Could read their names:

Albion

The Medora

Elizabeth Hughes

C. H. Appleton

Coldstream

St. George

Valhalla

These were the famine ships,

Known as the coffin ships.

Between 1845 and 1850

These ships had serviced Galway in a desperate bid to save the starving, dying population.

I shook my head and the visions evaporated.

I felt a speech or some sort of spoken words would be fitting on the day I finally

Dropped the hammer.

My mind resonated with the most powerful death passage in movie history

. . . Roy Batty (Rutger Hauer) in *Blade Runner*:

"I've seen things like

You people wouldn't believe:

Attack ships on fire off the shoulder of Orion;

I watched c-beams glitter in the dark near the the Tannhäuser Gate.

All those moments

Will be lost

Like tears in rain.

Time to die."

The image of Roy Batty dying in the rain seemed so damn apt.

If you want to tear the very heart from your chest. Watch the clip

On YouTube.

I had allowed these words, this image, to sear into my psyche. I almost lived the end of *Under the Volcano* where they dump a dead dog into the hole after the body of the consul.

On the edge of the Claddagh Basin, I met Cathy. The woman whose daughter, Serena-May, had died on my watch.

In a life-affirming book, the type of shite that would get you on *Oprah*, Cathy would have embraced me and cooed,

"I love and forgive you."
Right?
She spat in my face,
Cursed,
"May you never have a day's peace."

Joanna Taylor, in an essay on film noir, suggested Ray Batty aligned himself with Wagner's Tannhäuser, a character who has fallen from grace with men and with God. Both are characters whose faith is beyond their control.

Got a message from Sister Maeve. She had located the man and boy. They had indeed been on Aran but questions from locals had them depart fast. The man had seemed, in the words of the locals,

. . . to be a little overaffectionate to the boy.

Yeah, right.

So the fuck legged it.

Now the chances were good he might still be in Galway. I called Owen Daglish, a disgruntled Guard, still on the force but very bitter with the powers that wanted a new type of policeman.

Meaning, not Owen.

He was old school.

Translate, he never had a suspect who didn't respond to the lesson of the hurley. As in, beat the living shite out of him without leaving the marks. Did I concur with this form of faux vigilantism?

Pretty much.

You wanted something from Owen, you had to buy him drink.

Lots of.

We met in Garavan's, the barman greeting,

"Jack, I heard you were in jail."

People heard all sorts of shit about me, never . . . ever . . . like . . . you joined the Samaritans

Or

Even

. . . you volunteer at Age Concern.

Nope.

It was always down and dirty.

And,

Whisper it,

Shabby.

Some of it was even based on truth.

Owen was already working on a pint, chaser riding point. He looked

. . . fucked.

Par for the course for a Guard on the way out and down. He was wearing what had once been euphemistically termed a wax jacket. Now it not only was non-wax but barely resembled a jacket. Some guys, they let three days go unshaven and get that

Don Johnson

Jason Statham

Vibe.

Others

Look

Vagrant.

Guess which Owen was.

He said,

"Stanley Reed? Supposedly he and his son have some history."

You had to appreciate his straight down to biz attitude. The barman brought a refill for Owen and a pint and chaser for me. No words were exchanged. This is the almost sacred ritual between good bar guys and valued customers.

Valued, as in

They tip.

A lot.

I said,

"Tell me."

"Mr. Reed has a sheet of sex offenses as long as a tax bill. The boy, Daniel, is actually a nephew but UK cops believe he is indeed, if you'll pardon my French . . ."

Pause.

. . . "Diddling the poor lad."

Jesus.

He produced a sheet of paper, said,

"This cost, Jack."

I passed over an envelope, laden with euros. He flicked through the notes, went,

"Humph."

Signifying nothing, nothing at all. He said,

"I don't expect them to last long there as the Guards are attempting to get an English warrant."

Delay and deferral, the name of the bureaucratic game. I asked,

"Can't they hold him on some pretext?"

He sighed, sank the pint, said,

"See, Jack, the fuckup with the Grammarian, they are not rushing to arrests so much."

He played with his empty glass and I signaled for a refill. He added,

"That whole clusterfuck, Ridge is for the high jump."

"What?"

He gave a bitter laugh, said,

"Someone has to carry the shit can and she's the designated driver."

I said,

"I owe his aunt some money for supposedly trying to prove Wilson was innocent."

He examined the fresh pint for flaws, found none, said,

"Don't think she'll much care by this stage. The mad bastard is no longer an issue."

He glanced at the paper in my hand, asked,

"What are you planning to do with that, Jack?"

I smiled, malice in my soul, said,

"Something fucking biblical."

He touched his glass against mine, said,

"We expect nothing less."

"Suddenly the years catch up with the old swan and it glides to a small fern protected by reeds. Laying its majestic head on its sad breast, it emits a tiny shriek and lets the water take it."

Finally tracked down Em, by using her

   . . . greenhell@gmail.com

Tag.

We met in McSwiggans and she showed up in Chrissie Hynde mode. Jet-black hair, kohl makeup, a tiny gold guitar brooch on her black leather jacket, and, if I'm not mistaken, a ripped Vivienne Westwood black T-shirt. It said on the front

   . . . this is a ripped Westwood T-shirt.

I was post Guard 1970.

As in item 1834, black 501s, and a sour expression. I said,

   "You've covered all the icons there I think."

She struck a pose, said,

   "Brass in pocket."

For a vague tense moment, it seemed we might hug but it evaporated. She shouted,

   "Yo, barkeep, service before the fall."

Then she leaned over and gave me a forceful puck in the chest, said,

   "You shithead, how many months are you gone under the radar?"

We ordered a couple of longnecks and got the look from the barmaid. Em snapped at her,

"We're down-home folks so get to it."

She did.

Reluctantly.

She gave me a searching look and you know you have been full measured and assessed when an Irishwoman does that.

And

Found wanting.

She said,

"You're different, Jack."

Death sentence will do that I guess. Did I share?

Did I fuck?

Went with,

"How's your mom?"

Not *mum* but this fake schmaltzy affectionate term. She managed to fast convert a grimace to a smile, said,

"I bought her a car."

Before I could comment, she continued,

"Nice breezy little yellow convertible, the color to match her cowardly soul."

Phew.

I tried,

"Convertible? Not so sure that is really how would I put it, an Irish car."

"How astute, Jack. Turns out the brakes had been tampered with."

What?

She gave her smile of utter innocence she kept for utter lies, said,

"Went off the road near Silverstrand, I so hope she got to see the beach before . . . She broke her back and um . . . her neck too, I think, but who's keeping count, eh?"

Of all our failings, loss for words isn't something we Irish can be accused of.

I was lost for words. She leaned over, touched my arm, said in a down-home tone,

"Don't sweat it, big fellah."

I wanted to strangle her. Finally, I tried,

"Why on God's awful earth would you want to . . ."

Grasped for a word.

Got . . .

". . . *share*

Such utter madness with me?"

She drained her drink, seemed intent on getting wasted in jig time, said,

"I like you, Jack, even though you broke into my apartment and I do want that golden gun returned. I like to hang with you."

Jesus.

She continued,

"And if I hang, you'll fucking hang right along with me."

I saw another drink had materialized before me and I took a long draft, considered my position.

Three months at best until curtains and what was still left, dare I say, *hanging*? There was the boy, and the man molesting him, so I went for the darkness. I mean, if you have a tame psycho in tow, why not utilize her?

I told her about Stanley Reed and Daniel and that I had their address. She pounced, near shouted,

"Shit, let's go waste the fucker now."

Well, you couldn't fault her enthusiasm. I said, in a measured tone,

"This one is personal. The guy kicked the living shite out of me and I kind of want to pay back."

Payback.

Revenge.

Retaliation.

These were the walls within which she lived. She asked,

"What do you want me to do?"

Outlined the plan and she clapped her hands, said,

"I could go all *Orphan Black*?"

"Discretion is the key here."

"Long as I get to dress up."

Then she paused, took a look at me, asked,

"What's different with you?"

She always had an uncanny ability to home in on things, so I went deflection, said,

"Must be cutting back on the booze."

Shook her head, then,

"Like you have an air of resignation. I was going to say surrender but that's not in the Taylor songbook."

Hmm.

I asked,

"So you and the Doc not an item anymore?"

She clinked the rim of her glass against her top teeth, a very irritating sound, said,

"I was just mind-fucking him."

"Why?"

She seemed genuinely puzzled at this, then,

"Because I could."

I said,

"Kind of cold."

She stood up, laid a wad of notes on the counter, said,

"He was a bore and, like, I gave the poor bollix a dash of color. Where's the downside?"

"I think he feels a bit of a loser."

She laughed, loudly, said,

"Jesus, he was always that. I just brought it into focus."

We set our plan for the boy and man and I asked her, earnestly,

"Can I rely on you not to fuck this up?"

She laughed, said,

"Oh, fuckups. Surely you have the lock on that, Jackie-boy."

She had a point.

Back at my apartment, being under a death date, I could afford to be, if not magnanimous, then at least courteous. I had a bottle of sour mash, not easy to find in Galway but at McCambridge's, the shop where the remnants of Anglo-Irish still lingered, you could find almost any hooch, at a price.

When it was busy, it was not unlike Ascot.

Hooray Henrys

In their faux Barbour coats.

Horsey women with sunglasses perched on their heads.

Dodgy solicitors dodging their dodgier clients.

And the new impoverished frat boys, once billionaires on paper and now not able to rub tuppence on a mortgaged tombstone.

The manageress, a rarity in Irish young women — she had a real accent, not the pseudo fucked American of Valley girls. She greeted,

"Jack, howyah?"

Not entirely sure why but that made me feel as if there are actually some things I might miss alongside breathing.

Thus armed, I knocked on Doc's door. Took a bang or three but finally he opened the door a crack. Muttered,

"I gave at the office."

I pushed my way in, proclaiming,

"Your time of whinging is up. She dumped you, get over it."

He looked . . .

. . . fucking dreadful.

Only women can pull off the worn dressing gown look. And certainly no man of my generation can, if you'll pardon the pun, carry off a box of tissues.

It's just fucking gay.

So shoot me, the PC brigade.

His unshaven face looked like somebody squatted in his face and had bested all eviction notices. Oddly, his apartment was immaculate. I had noticed this before with Em's mother, the lethal drinking coupled with an obsessive need to keep outward things in order, as if the

324

chaos of the mind might be tempered by a severity of order in the surroundings.

Or, fuck,

. . . maybe they were just tidy.

I proffered the bottle and he asked, his voice a croak, a sure sign the vocal cords are out of use,

"We're going American?"

I said,

"Seems to work for the government."

He went to the kitchen, brought back two heavy tumblers, said,

"Part of a wedding gift."

I lamely went,

"Oh."

Deep, eh?

He said,

"There were six but I smashed them to smithereens to accessorize my new existence."

He poured the booze and, as I looked around to sit, I tried,

"I'm sorry about you and . . . Em."

He knocked back the shot like a good un, sneered,

"Don't be a prick. You're not sorry, not one fucking bit. You think it's good enough for an old codger to get stiffed."

Jesus.

I said,

"Well, in that case, tough shit."

And . . .

He laughed.

We sat glaring at each other for a minute, then he said, cold voice,

"If there is nothing else, I need to get back to staring out the window."

I stood and tried to come up with something Dr. Phil might provide.

Nothing.

I moved to the door and said,

"Hang in there, summer is coming."

Fuck.

He gave a grimace, said,

"I've reached the tunnel at the end of the light."

How come the word

      A

        B

          B

            R

              E

                V

                  I

                    A

                      T

                        I

                          O

                            N

                              is so long?

I had asked Em to pose as a Child Services officer and, if she could, to leave Reed's house with the child Daniel.

If anyone could, she was the best bet. Five the next evening, I waited outside the house that Stanley Reed rented with the boy. Sure enough, a black Audi rolled up and out marched Em.

Dressed in a dark power suit, carrying a heavy briefcase, her hair severely tied back, and her face like the wrath of God, she strode up to the door and banged loudly. Stan opened and she bulldozed her way past him. I lit a cig, settled in to wait, but, to my amazement, the door opened after ten minutes and out came Em, leading the boy, who looked bewildered. Stan was waving his arms and Em turned sharply on a heel, got right up to his face, and read some riot act

. . . because he backed off.

She got Daniel into the car then pulled smartly out of there. I barely saw her face but I could have sworn I saw the beginning of a smile.

Okay, showtime.

I went around to the back of the house, jimmied the back door easily — no security but, then, when the monster is within, who needs locks? Into a cluttered hall, took a deep breath, took the revolver from my jacket, moved forward. Could hear Stanley screaming on the phone to, I presume, Child Services.

". . . What the bloody hell do you mean you didn't assign anybody, this is outrageous."

I tapped him lightly on the shoulder.

He whirled around and I used the butt of the gun, broke his nose. He fell backward, the phone clattering on the floor. I said,

"That is a Galway hello."

I picked up the phone, a voice leaking from it, like this:

". . . Hello? Hello? Is anyone there?"

I said,

"Please hold, your call is important to us. For customer service, press 1."

Reed was holding his nose, blood cascading along his impressively white shirt. He managed to focus, accused,

"I know you."

I gave him my best smile, a blend of bitterness and devilry, said,

"You probably recall me best on the ground with your fucking shoe in my face."

He said,

"The ferry."

Then tried to figure out how to join the dots. Shaking his head, he said,

"I'm guessing the lady from Child Services wasn't
. . . from them?"

"Not much gets by you, unless you count the broken
nose."

He looked around, weighing his options, then,

"So what's the plan, hotshot? You planning to shoot
me?"

I pulled the hammer back, not for show as much as I
relished the symbolism of that solid clunk, like a candle
you light, thinking it carries significance. I said,

"Well, it is real simple. You leave town or you stay
and see what I will do next."

Not sure what he would do but laughter wasn't part
of any scenarios. There was no way in hell this pervert
was leaving the house but I wanted to fuck with him, let
him believe he had a chance to bail.

He laughed.

Said,

"Daniel, the boy?"

I nodded.

"You think I . . . snatched him?"

Superciliousness leaked all over his tone and the
broken nose added a shade of bravado he was adopting.
I said,

"All I know is you are done with him."

He stared at me as if I were a moron, asked,

"Shit, you really don't get it, do you?"

I moved toward him and he raised his voice, near
screamed,

"Yah dumb fuck, they sold him."

Stopped me and I tried to focus. He pushed,

"That's right, Sherlock. I paid cash money for the little honey."

I felt my world tilt and a dangerous mist danced before my eyes. I said,

"You really need to shut the fuck up right now."

And he laughed.

Sneered.

"A day or two, tops! I'll buy another, hell, maybe twins." Adopted a cockney accent — "Buy one, get the second free!"

My mind in hyperdrive, I raised the gun to his face.

"Go on,"

He taunted.

"I dare you."

Storm clouds your judgment, and herein
Lies
    the
       Very
          Essence
              of
                 the
                     Emerald
                        Lie.

I phoned Ridge. The doctor had gotten in touch with me again and implied that maybe . . . just perhaps . . .

His diagnosis was off the mark a tad.

Now did I go and tear his fucking head off?

Or

Buy him a crate of Jameson?

No. I rolled the dice.

Didn't go to hear yet another verdict, decided to act as if I was still under the death sentence.

Why?

Because I was tired, in every area that weariness can touch.

I met Ridge in Garavan's and completely out of character, she ordered a large vodka, slimline tonic. I went with the Jay. She was dressed in a soft green sweater. You might even stretch and suggest, *emerald*?

White jeans that dazzled in their brightness, but there the shine ended.

She looked fatigued.

Well, fucked, actually.

I said,

"You look terrific."

Got the stare.

She said,

"This Emily? Nothing about her is kosher."

I laughed, mimicked,

"Kosher? Seriously? From a west of Ireland woman?"

She slammed her glass on the table, her very empty glass, said,

"One way or another, I will get her, and if you are any part of that, it will be a joy to do you too."

I considered telling her my fifty-fifty chance of being out of the game. Would I get a break, some sympathy, maybe even a shot at repairing our tattered friendship?

I said,

"I have not been feeling well."

She was on her feet, spittle leaking from her mouth. She fumed,

"Well? Are you kidding me? You haven't been well for twenty years and what on earth are you telling me for?"

I tried,

"Because of our, um, you know, history?"

She gave a short bitter laugh, moved to the door, then, as parting,

"You could die tomorrow, I could give a fucking toss."

I sat completely still, then muttered,

"All in all, I think it went okay."

The storm.

the storm).

I dressed as if my life depended on it.

You might term that sarcasm if I had any juice left. I put on my Garda all-weather coat and, underneath, a thick white Aran sweater. I didn't want to be cold.

Dead is one thing, but cold? No, fuck that. The oft-threatened storm was blowing hard and bitter. The streets would be deserted.

Good.

I put a bottle of Jameson in my right pocket. The gun carefully in my left pocket. It is the attention to the little things that make the scene. I wore my Doc Martens, scuffed and worn like my wasting, withered soul. I looked at my reflection in the mirror, said,

"Dying to meet you."

I was tempted to wear a snazzy emerald scarf that Emily had left behind. Give me that raffish rakish air. Said,

"Guess that would be like

. . . An

Emerald

Lie."

You think?

As I strolled down the quiet streets, the wind howled like embellishment and not a busker to its name. A man emerged from the small alley that runs beside Eason's bookshop. He was huddling against the storm, stopped, greeted,

"Jack? Jack fucking Taylor?"

I wanted to say,

"As I live and breathe."

But, you know, too facile.

He asked,

"You going to a funeral?"

Now I laughed, said,

"You are a man of deep discernment."

He went,

"What?"

I moved past him and he shouted,

"How are you fixed?"

Meaning, have you money to spare, to lend or give?

I handed him my wallet and he went,

"Is this a joke?"

I said,

"With a killer line."

Nimmo's pier was at the very end of the Claddagh, overlooking the bay, and not one swan to be seen. During fierce weather, you would see swans huddled against the walls of the dock. Not a one.

Like the monkeys deserting Gibraltar perhaps?

I managed, despite the ferocious wind, to reach the end of the pier and braced myself against the wall. One of the things I have loved about cinema is the long tracking shot. I imagined a lens framing a small figure, stark against the granite . . .

And then the camera pans away, higher and higher, like desperate hope, showing a futile figure in a futile coat, signifying nothing of note or comment.

It amazes me that suicide has been called a cowardly act. Man, it takes real balls to even walk right to the precipice.

Some lines moved in my mind

Not with a bang

But a whimper.

Shouted,

"I don't fucking do whimper."

My words caught on the wind, framed and cast among the rocks that were sentries to the Atlantic Ocean.

I nearly laughed as I realized I'd forgotten to take a drink. I took the gun out of my pocket, let it rest against my leg, thumbed the hammer back, relishing yet again the comforting clunk of the action. Like an apprentice Zippo.

I continued to look toward America and felt the gun tremble a little. Would I sneak up on myself, so to speak, the left hand not knowing what the right planned?

I asked,

"Is that it?"

And

Answered,

"On the other hand . . ."